"Harlequin Desire—
lush, sensual reads guaranteed to take me away!"
—*USA TODAY* Bestselling Author Catherine Mann

Look for all six
Special 30th Anniversary Collectors' Editions
from some of our most popular authors.

TEMPTED BY HER INNOCENT KISS
by Maya Banks
with "Never Too Late" by Brenda Jackson

BEHIND BOARDROOM DOORS
by Jennifer Lewis
with "The Royal Cousin's Revenge"
by Catherine Mann

THE PATERNITY PROPOSITION
by Merline Lovelace
with "The Sheik's Virgin" by Susan Mallery

A TOUCH OF PERSUASION
by Janice Maynard
with "A Lover's Touch" by Brenda Jackson

A FORBIDDEN AFFAIR
by Yvonne Lindsay
with "For Love or Money" by Elizabeth Bevarly

CAUGHT IN THE SPOTLIGHT
by Jules Bennett
with "Billionaire's Baby" by Leanne Banks

* * *

Find Harlequin Desire on Facebook,
www.facebook.com/HarlequinDesire,
or on Twitter, @desireeditors!

Dear Reader,

How cool to be a part of the 30th anniversary celebration for Desire! I'm a longtime fan of Harlequin books, all the way back to high school. In fact, I often tell people about the one time I got in trouble as a teen, when my science teacher caught me reading a Harlequin tucked inside my textbook. (I finished reading the book in after-school detention.) Little did I know then that I was preparing for my career writing romance novels!

Even after writing more than forty books of my own, I still enjoy curling up with the latest Harlequin Desire title and letting the outside world fade away for a few hours. And that's one of the things I enjoy most about a Desire read—the guaranteed "take me away" quality. It's like a fantasy vacation—without breaking the bank or missing work the next morning.

I'm thrilled that my short story "The Royal Cousin's Revenge" has been included as a bonus feature for the anniversary celebration. I hope Javier and Victoria's story sweeps you away for a "minivacation" at their royal family's island retreat. To read more about Javier's aristocratic relatives, check out my Rich, Rugged and Royal series. *The Maverick Prince, His Thirty-Day Fiancée* and *His Heir, Her Honor* are all still available from Harlequin Desire in ebook form.

Happy anniversary, Harlequin Desire!

Cheers,

Catherine Mann

JENNIFER LEWIS

BEHIND BOARDROOM DOORS

Special thanks and acknowledgment to Jennifer Lewis for her contribution to the Dynasties: The Kincaids miniseries.

ISBN-13: 978-0-373-73157-2

Recycling programs for this product may not exist in your area.

This edition published by arrangement with Harlequin Books S.A.

For questions and comments about the quality of this book please contact us at Customer_eCare@Harlequin.ca.

www.Harlequin.com

Printed in U.S.A.

CONTENTS

Books by Jennifer Lewis

Harlequin Desire

†*Claiming His Royal Heir* #2105
Behind Boardroom Doors #2144
†*The Prince's Pregnant Bride* #2082
†*At His Majesty's Convenience* #2094

Silhouette Desire

The Boss's Demand #1812
Seduced for the Inheritance #1830
Black Sheep Billionaire #1847
Prince of Midtown #1891
**Millionaire's Secret Seduction* #1925
**In the Argentine's Bed* #1931
**The Heir's Scandalous Affair* #1938
The Maverick's Virgin Mistress #1977
The Desert Prince #1993
Bachelor's Bought Bride #2012

*The Hardcastle Progeny
†Royal Rebels

Other titles by this author available in ebook format.

JENNIFER LEWIS

has been dreaming up stories for as long as she can remember and is thrilled to be able to share them with readers. She has lived on both sides of the Atlantic and worked in media and the arts before she grew bold enough to put pen to paper. She would love to hear from readers at jen@jenlewis.com. Visit her website at www.jenlewis.com.

Dear Reader,

I'm thrilled to be a part of Desire's 30th anniversary celebration. I still remember the first time I discovered Desire. I was working in midtown Manhattan, around the corner from the Donnell Library. On my lunch breaks I often headed to the library looking for something to read, and before long I noticed the big rack of series romance novels. I don't remember which book I picked up first, but it didn't take me long to get hooked.

I loved the strong, savvy characters in every Desire, and the interesting mix of settings. I looked forward to plunging into each new romance and following the ups and downs of the couple's road to their happy ending. I also enjoyed the short length of the stories, which allowed me to ride the whole rollercoaster in a day.

Eventually I grew daring enough to try my hand at writing, though it took many years before I honed my craft enough to bear the Desire logo. This book is my fourteenth Desire and I hope you enjoy Brooke and RJ's romance!

Happy reading,

Jennifer Lewis

For Pippa, international pony of mystery
and cherished member of our family

* * *

Don't miss a single book in this series!

Dynasties: The Kincaids
New money. New passions. Old secrets.

Sex, Lies and the Southern Belle by Kathie DeNosky
What Happens in Charleston... by Rachel Bailey
Behind Boardroom Doors by Jennifer Lewis
On the Verge of I Do by Heidi Betts
One Dance with the Sheikh by Tessa Radley
A Very Private Merger by Day Leclaire

BEHIND BOARDROOM DOORS

Jennifer Lewis

One

"There is one good thing about this situation." RJ Kincaid slammed his phone down on the conference table, his voice cracking with fury.

"What's that?" Brooke Nichols stared at her boss. She failed to see a bright side.

"Now we know things cannot possibly get any worse." His eyes flashed and he leaned forward in his chair. The other staff in the meeting sat like statues. "My calls to the prosecutor's office, the police, the courts, the state senator—have all been ignored."

He stood and marched around the table. "The Kincaid family is under siege and they're firing on us from all angles." Tall and imposing at the best of times, with bold features, dark hair and smoky slate-blue eyes, RJ now looked like a general striding into battle. "And my mother, Elizabeth Winthrop Kincaid, the finest woman in Charleston, will be spending tonight behind bars like a common criminal."

He let out a string of curses that made Brooke shrink into her chair. She'd worked for RJ for five years and she'd never seen him like this. Normally he was the most easygoing man you could meet, never rattled by even the most intense negotiations, with time for everyone and a nonchalant approach to life.

Of course that was before his father's murder and the revelation that his privileged and entitled existence was founded on lies.

RJ walked over to his brother Matthew. "You're the director of new business—is there any new business?"

Matthew inhaled. They both knew the answer. Even some of their most stalwart clients had fled the company in the aftermath of the scandal. "There is the Larrimore account."

"Yes, I suppose we do have one new account to hang our hopes on. Greg, how are the books looking?" RJ strode around to the CFO and for a moment she thought he was going to collar him.

Mild-mannered Greg shrank into his chair. "As you know, we're experiencing challenges—"

"Challenges!" RJ cut him off, raising his hands in the air in a dramatic gesture. "That's one way of looking at it. A challenge is an opportunity for growth, a time to rise up and seize opportunity, to embrace change."

He turned and walked back across the room. Everyone sat rigid in their chairs, probably praying he wouldn't accost them.

"But what I see here is a company on the brink of going under." RJ shoved a hand through his thick, dark hair. His handsome features were hard with anger. "And all of you are just sitting in your chairs taking notes as if we're at some garden party. Get up and get out there and do something, for Chrissakes!"

No one moved an inch. Brooke rose from her chair, unable to stop herself. "Um..." She had to get him out of here. He was acting like a jerk and if he continued like this he'd do himself permanent harm in the company.

"Yes, Brooke?" He turned to face her, and lifted an eyebrow. His eyes met hers and a jolt of energy surged in her blood.

"I need to speak to you outside." She picked up her laptop and headed for the door, heart pounding. He could probably fire her on the spot in his current mood, but she wasn't doing her job if she let him insult and harangue employees who were already under a lot of pressure and stress through no fault of their own.

"I'm sure it can wait." He frowned and gestured to the gathered meeting.

"Just for a moment. Please." She continued toward the door, hoping he'd follow.

"Apparently my assistant's need to consult with me in private is more urgent than the imminent collapse of The Kincaid Group, and the imprisonment of my mother. Since it's the end of the day I'm sure you also have better places to be. Meeting dismissed."

RJ moved to the door in time to hold it open for her. A wave of heat and adrenaline rose inside her as she passed him, her arm almost brushing against his. He closed the door and followed her out. In the hush of the carpeted hallway Brooke almost lost her nerve. "In your office, please."

"I don't have time to loll about in my office. My mother's in the county jail in case you hadn't noticed."

Brooke reminded herself his rudeness was the result of extreme stress. "Trust me. It's important." Her own firm tone surprised her. She walked ahead into the spacious corner office with views of the Charleston waterfront. The sunset cast a warm amber glow over the water reflected on the walls in moving patterns. "Come on in."

RJ sauntered into the room, then crossed his arms. "Happy now?"

"Sit down." She closed the door and locked it.

"What?"

Her resolve faltered as her boss glared at her.

"On the couch." She pointed to it, in case he'd forgotten where it was. She almost blushed at the way it sounded as she said it. What a lovelorn secretary's fantasy! But this situation was serious. "I'm going to pour you a whiskey and you're going to drink it."

He didn't move. "Have you lost your mind?"

"No, but you're beginning to lose yours and you need to step back and take a deep breath before you damage your reputation. You can't talk to employees like that, no matter what the circumstances. Now sit." She pointed at the sofa again.

A stunned RJ lowered himself onto it.

Brooke poured three fingers of whisky into a crystal tumbler with shaking hands. Everything really did seem to be going to hell in a handbasket for RJ. Until now he'd faced each disaster with composure, but apparently he'd reached his breaking point.

Their fingers touched as she handed him the glass, and she cursed the subtle buzz of awareness that always haunted her around RJ. "Here, this will settle your nerves."

"My nerves are just fine." He took a sip. "It's everything else that's screwed up. The police can't really believe my mother killed my father!"

He took a long swig, which made Brooke wince. She bit her lip. The pained expression on his handsome face tugged at her heart. "We both know it's impossible, and they'll figure that out."

"Will they?" RJ raised a dark brow and peered up at her. "What if they don't? What if this is the first of many long nights in jail for her?" He shuddered visibly and took another swig. "It kills me that I can't protect her from this."

"I know. And you're still grieving the death of your father."

"Not just his literal death." RJ stared at the floor. "The death of everything I thought I knew about him."

She and RJ had never discussed the scandalous revelations about the Kincaid family, but they were both aware she knew all the details—along with everyone else in Charleston. They'd been splashed all over the local media every day since his father's murder on December 30th. It was now March.

"Another family." He growled the words like a curse. "Another son, born before me." He shook his head. "All my life I was Reginald Kincaid, Jr. Proud son and heir and all I wanted to do was follow in my father's footsteps. Little did I know they'd been wandering off into some other woman's house, to sleep with her and raise her children, too."

He glanced up, and his pain-filled gaze stole her

breath. It killed her to see him suffering like this. If only she could soothe his hurt and anger.

"I'm so sorry." It was all she could manage. What could she say? "I'm sure he loved you. You could see it in his face when he looked at you." She swallowed. "I bet he wished things were different, and that he could have at least told you before he died."

"He had plenty of time to tell me. I'm thirty-six years old, for Chrissakes. Was he waiting until I hit fifty?" RJ rose to his feet and crossed the room, whiskey splashing in the glass. "That's what hurts the most. That he didn't confide in me. All the time we spent together, all those long hours fishing or hunting, walking through the woods with guns. We talked about everything under the sun—except that he was living a lie."

RJ tugged at his tie with a finger and loosened his collar. Recent events had given him an air of gravitas that he'd never had before. The strain hardened his noble features and gave his broad shoulders the appearance of carrying the weight of the world.

Brooke longed to take him in her arms and give him a reassuring hug. But that would *not* be a good idea. "You're doing a great job of keeping the family together and the company afloat."

"Afloat!" RJ let out a harsh laugh. "It would be a real problem for a shipping company if it couldn't stay afloat." His eyes twinkled with humor for a split second. "But at the rate we're losing clients we'll be belly up in the bay before the year is out if I don't turn things around. For every new client Matthew brings in, we're losing two old ones. And I don't even have a free hand to guide the company. My father—in his infinite wisdom—saw fit to give his illegitimate son forty-five percent of the company and only leave me a measly nine percent."

Brooke grimaced. That did seem the cruelest act of all. RJ had devoted his entire working life to The Kincaid Group. He'd been executive vice president almost since he left college, and everyone—including him—assumed he'd one day be president and CEO. Until his father had all but left the company to a son no one knew about. "I suppose he did that because he felt guilty about keeping Jack secret all these years."

"As well he might." RJ marched back across the room and took another swig of whiskey. "Except he didn't seem to think about how much it would hurt the rest of us. Even all five of us Kincaids together don't have a majority vote. Ten percent of the stock is owned by some mystery person we can't seem to find. If Jack Sinclair gains control over the missing ten percent he'll get to decide how to run The Kincaid Group and the rest of us have to go along with it or ship out. I'm seriously considering doing the latter."

"Leaving the company?" She couldn't believe it. Selfish thoughts about her own job disappearing almost toppled her concern for RJ.

"Why not? It's not mine to run. I'm just another cog in the machine. That's not what my dad groomed me for or what I want for myself." He slammed the empty glass down on a table. "Maybe I'll leave Charleston for good."

"Calm down, RJ." Brooke poured another three fingers of pungent whiskey into the glass. Right now it seemed a good idea to get him too drunk to go anywhere at all. "It's early days yet. Nothing will be decided about the company until the shareholders' meeting and, until then, everyone's counting on you to steer the ship through these rough waters."

"I love all your nautical lingo." He flashed a wry grin as he took the glass. "I knew there was a good reason I hired you."

"That and my excellent typing skills."

"Typing—pah. You could run this company if you put your mind to it. You're not just organized and efficient, you're good with people. You've managed to talk me back off the ledge today, and I thank you for it." He took another sip. The whiskey was certainly doing its job. Already the hard edge of despair and anger had softened.

Now was not the time to mention that she had applied for a management job, and been turned down. She didn't know if RJ was behind that, or if he even knew.

"I didn't want you to upset people any more than they already are." She pushed a hand through her hair. "Everyone's temper is running high and we need to work together. The last thing you want is for key employees to quit and make things worse in the run-up to the shareholders' meeting."

"You're right, as usual, my lovely Brooke."

Her eyes widened. Obviously the whiskey was going straight to his head. Still, she couldn't help the funny warm feeling his words generated inside her, almost like a shot of whiskey to her core.

"The most important thing right now is to find your dad's murderer." She tried to distract herself from RJ's melting gaze. "Then your mom won't be under suspicion."

"I've hired a private investigator." RJ peered into

his glass. "I told him I'll pay for twenty-four hours in the day and he shouldn't stop until he finds the truth." He looked up at her. "Of course I told him to start with the Sinclair brothers."

Brooke nodded. Jack Sinclair sounded like a man with an ax to grind, though her vision could be skewed by the fact that he'd inherited her boss's birthright. She hadn't met Jack or his half brother Alan. "They must be angry your dad kept them secret all these years."

"Yup. Resentment." RJ sat down on the sofa again. "I'm beginning to know what that feels like."

"Very understandable." Her chest ached with emotion. She wished she could bear some of the burden for him. "This whole situation came out of nowhere for you."

"Not to mention my mom." He shook his head. "Though sometimes I wonder if she knew. She didn't seem as surprised as the rest of us."

Brooke swallowed. Elizabeth Kincaid would have had at least some motivation for the murder if she'd known about her husband's adultery. And she had seen her in the office on the night of the murder. She shook the thought from her brain. There was no way such a quiet and gentle person could fire a bullet at another human, even her cheating husband. "Let me pour you some more."

She brought the bottle over to the sofa and leaned down to fill RJ's glass. The whiskey sloshed in the bottle as he stuck out a strong arm and pulled her roughly onto the sofa with him. She let out a tiny shriek as her hips settled into the soft leather next to his.

"I appreciate the company, Brooke. I guess I needed someone to talk to." His arm had now settled across her shoulders, his big hand wrapped around her upper arm. She could hardly breathe. And when she did his warm, masculine scent assaulted her senses and raised her blood pressure.

RJ settled into the sofa a little, caressing her shoulder with his hand. Heat bloomed under his fingers, through her thin blouse. She still held the whiskey bottle and wondered if she should pour from it, or if he'd had enough. He answered the question by taking it from her with his free hand, and putting it on the floor along with his glass. His hand then settled on her thigh, where she could feel the warmth of his palm through her smart gray skirt. Her heart quickened when he turned to look at her.

RJ's expression was one of intense concentration. He seemed to be examining her face like she was a table of container ship sailings. "I never noticed how green your eyes are."

Brooke had a sudden urge to roll those eyes. How many women had he used that line on? RJ was famous throughout the Southeast as a Most Eligible Bachelor and had enjoyed his single status as long as she'd known him. "Some people would call them gray." Was she really sitting almost in RJ's lap talking about her eyes, or was this some kind of manic dream?

"They'd be wrong." Again his expression was deadly serious. "But lately I'm learning that people are wrong a lot of the time." His gaze fell to her mouth. Her lips parted slightly and she pressed them back together. "I'm having to question a lot of my assumptions about the world."

"Sometimes that's good." She spoke softly, wondering if she'd said the wrong thing. Sitting this close to

RJ was dangerous. Arousal already crept through her limbs and strange parts of her were starting to tingle.

"I suppose so." RJ frowned. "Though it doesn't make life any easier."

Poor RJ. He was used to being the golden child, his entire life mapped out at birth and his every need taken care of before he could even voice it.

"Sometimes challenges can make us stronger." It was hard to form sensible thoughts with his arm around her shoulder and his other hand on her knee. She could feel the power of his sturdy body right through her clothes. Part of her wanted to stand up and go organize the papers on his desk. The other part wanted to wrap her arms around his neck and…

RJ's lips crushed over hers in a hot, whiskey-scented kiss that banished all thought. Her body melted against his and she felt her fingers do what they'd wanted all along—roam into his stiff white shirt and the hard, hot muscle beneath.

His hands caressed her, making her skin hum with arousal. Her nipples thickened and a powerful wave of heat rose in her belly. RJ's raw hunger for affection—for help—gave urgency to his touch. She could feel how badly he needed her, right now, here in his arms.

She kissed him back with equal force, affection for him overpowering any more sensible urges. She wanted to heal his hurt, to make him feel better, and right now she almost felt that was within her power. Emotions surged within her. She'd adored RJ almost since the day she met him and his strength under adversity only made her admire him more. She'd never dared imagine for a single second that he'd return her feelings.

Their kiss deepened and heated and for a moment she thought they'd fuse and become one, then RJ pulled back gently. "Brooke, you're an amazing woman."

His soft sigh contained a thick aroma of all those fingers of whiskey she'd poured him. Would he regret this in the morning? Still, hearing him call her an amazing woman stirred something powerful inside her. Was this the beginning of a totally new phase in their relationship? Maybe they'd start dating and she'd be able to help him negotiate the minefield of his life and come happily out the other side with him—arm in arm. His arms felt fabulous around her right now.

Or would she remember this as the moment she destroyed her hard-earned career at The Kincaid Group and permanently alienated her boss by getting him drunk and compromising their professional relationship? A ball of fear burst open like a mold spore inside her.

What was she doing? She'd gotten him drunk, then let him kiss her. It was all her fault, even she could see that.

RJ stroked her cheek and she fought a sudden urge to nuzzle against him like a cat. Was it so wrong to give him the affection and comfort he craved? Again, violins and visions of a rose-scented courtship hummed in her mind. She was strong enough to help him through this. Her own background had made her a resilient person.

RJ caressed her, taking in the curve of her breast with his fingers then trailing over her thigh. The musky scent of him filled her senses for a second as his lips met hers again and kissed her softly.

Cigar smoke clung to his suit from the long business lunch he'd hosted at a local restaurant, and mingled rather intoxicatingly with the whiskey. Everything about RJ seemed delicious to her right now. She wanted to wrap herself up in him and stay there forever.

But he withdrew again, leaving her lips stinging. Then he frowned and pushed a hand through his hair as if wondering what he was doing.

An icy finger of doubt slid down Brooke's back. Perhaps that smoky smell came from the smoldering ruin of her career and reputation. Instinct pushed her to her feet, which wasn't easy with her knees reduced to wobbly jelly. "Maybe it's time to get out of here. It's after seven."

RJ leaned his head back against the sofa, eyes closed. "I'm beat. I don't think I can take another step today."

"I'll call you a cab." She certainly didn't want him driving with all that whiskey in him. He didn't live far away, but driving or walking him home didn't seem like such a great idea, either. If he invited her in, she wasn't sure she could say no, and she knew she'd regret being that easy.

"Don't worry about me, Brooke. I'll sleep here on the sofa. I've done it many times before. If I wake up in the middle of the night I'll go through some of the paperwork I need to read."

"You'll wake up sore."

"I'll be fine." Already he was sinking into the sofa, eyes sleepy. "Go home and rest and I'll see you in the morning."

Brooke bit her lip. Somehow it hurt to be dismissed like this after their steamy kisses. What did she expect? That he'd want her by his side every moment from now on? Maybe after so much whiskey he'd already forgotten he even kissed her.

"What about dinner?"

"Not hungry," he murmured.

"There's half a plate of sandwiches in the fridge left over from a luncheon meeting today. I could get them for you."

"Stop trying to mother me, and go home." His tone was almost curt. Brooke swallowed and turned for the door. Then she noticed RJ had sat up again, head in his hands. "I can't believe my mom is in jail. It's just so wrong. I've never felt so powerless in my life."

Brooke walked back toward him. "She's a strong woman and she'll survive. You've done all you can for now and it won't help her if you worry yourself sick over it. Get some sleep so you'll be ready to make the most of tomorrow. You've got a company to save."

He blew out a hard breath. "You're right, Brooke, as usual. Thanks for everything."

Already he'd lain down, eyes closed. A fierce pang of tenderness for him ached in her chest. So tall and strong and proud and so anxious to go immediately into battle to save his mom. RJ was the kind of man any woman would adore. And she was only one among the many who did.

She slipped out of his office and closed the door, then picked up her jacket and bag from her own desk outside it. *Thanks for everything.* Was that his way of wrapping up the evening's events—memos typed, letters filed, kisses received. All in a day's work.

"Bye, Brooke."

She startled at the sound of her name. She'd totally forgotten there might still be other employees on the floor. Usually everyone was long gone by now, but PR assistant Lucinda was donning her jacket two cubicles away. Brooke wondered if her cheeks were flushed or her lips red. Surely there must be some telltale signs that she'd locked lips with her boss.

"Bye, Luce." She hurried for the elevator, hoping no one else would see her.

When the doors opened Joe from Marketing was inside. "What a day," he exhaled, as she stepped in. "This place is coming apart at the seams."

"No, it isn't." She bristled with indignation. "We're going through tough times but a year from now this will all be forgotten and the company will be back on top again."

Joe raised a sandy brow. "Really? If old Mrs. Kincaid did it I don't think the family reputation will recover. And it's sure looking like she did. I bet she's enjoying life as the merry widow now."

"She didn't do it." Still, a sliver of doubt wedged itself into her mind. Anyone could be pushed past their breaking point, and Elizabeth Kincaid had been pushed pretty far from the sound of it. "And don't go spreading rumors that she did. You'll make things worse."

"Are you going to report me to your boss?" He shifted his bag higher on his shoulder.

"No. He's got enough problems right now. He needs all of our support."

"You're like a wife to him, so supportive and attentive to his needs." His grin was less than reassuring. "If only we could all be as lucky as RJ."

She froze. Could he know something had happened between her and RJ? The doors opened and she stepped out with relief. "I'm not his wife."

Though maybe one day I could be. Fantasies already played at the edge of her mind. Dangerous fantasies. Dreams that could explode in her face and destroy her career and reputation.

Still it was hard not to let her imagination wander just a little....

Two

Brooke had a sleepless night. In the morning her hair was a mess and she had to whip out the curling iron to bring some life back to the limp brown locks brushing her shoulders. She applied her makeup carefully, wanting to look as beautiful as RJ had made her feel last night. Did she look different now that she'd kissed him?

Not really. At least her eyes weren't red from crying—yet. RJ would be able to blame his sudden enchantment with her on the whiskey she gave him. She, on the other hand, could blame only her years-long fascination with him. She'd fallen into his arms without a protest, and kissed him with passion that came from the heart.

She wore her smartest black suit. She'd bought it on sale at a fancy boutique, and with its well-cut designer lines it was something a rich girl would wear. She stood back and surveyed herself in the full-length mirror. Did she look like a potential girlfriend of RJ Kincaid?

She knew what her mom would say. *You have a nice figure, you should show it off more.* But that wasn't her style. Besides, the last thing she wanted was a man who only cared about her breasts and not her brain.

She donned her Burberry raincoat, a cherished consignment store find. She preferred a demure, somewhat conservative style that said, *I mean business.* She wanted people to take her seriously. She'd never flirted with RJ for a single instant, as her job meant far more to her than the prospect of a quick kiss and cuddle.

Fear licked around the edges of her brain. Would RJ be embarrassed by last night's indiscretions and find a way to shunt her aside? Her heart pounded as she walked into the Kincaid building.

Her throat dried as she stepped out of the elevator on their floor. How would she greet him? Would he be furious she'd made him drunk and landed them in a compromising position?

Maybe he wouldn't remember that he'd kissed her at all.

His office door was closed. Was RJ still in there sleeping on the sofa? She hung her coat with shaking hands and wiped sweaty palms on her skirt before approaching. She lifted her hand to knock, then hesitated.

Maybe she should wait for him to come out. He might have a major hangover he needed to sleep off. She turned and went to sit at her desk. She was always the first person in each morning. She liked to get her in-box dealt with before the phones started ringing.

Brooke checked her email, then pulled the mail from her tray and started to sort through it. But her eyes kept straying to the closed door. Was he still upset about his mom being jailed? Who wouldn't be? He could probably use a coffee and some breakfast.

She rose from her chair and approached the door again. She inhaled deeply and raised her hand—and the door opened.

The polite greeting she'd rehearsed fled her lips at the sight of RJ. She'd expected him to look rumpled and tired, but he didn't. Well groomed and wearing a perfectly pressed suit, he looked every inch the business titan his rivals feared.

"Morning, Brooke." His eyes twinkled with amusement.

"Morning." The word burst out fast and loud. Somehow he seemed even more gorgeous than usual. Maybe because she knew just how his mouth tasted in a kiss. She struggled to drag her mind back to practical matters. "Did you sleep okay?"

"I slept very well under the circumstances." He leaned against the door frame, eyes resting on her face. "It wasn't easy sleeping alone after that kiss." His deep blue eyes smoldered and his hushed tones carried more than a hint of suggestion.

Brooke bit her lip to stop a huge smile creeping across it. "For me either." Her admission was a relief. He wasn't trying to forget the kiss ever happened. "I'm glad you're feeling better this morning."

"I took your advice to heart. No sense weakening under pressure when I need all my energy to fight. Onwards and upwards, Brooke."

"That's the spirit." She let the big goofy smile widen her mouth. This was the RJ she'd grown to know and love. "What's first on the agenda this morning?"

He tilted his head slightly and lowered his voice. "The first thing on my agenda is to secure a date for tonight."

Brooke's heart almost stopped. Did he mean with her, or did he intend for her to call some strange woman and…

"Are you free after work this evening?"

"Yes," she stammered. "Yes, I am." How cool. Oh well, not like she had an image as a seductress to uphold.

"I'll make reservations and will pick you up at your place at seven-thirty."

"Great." Already her mind spun with worries about what to wear. Her cherished collection of business suits would be too stuffy for dinner and she didn't have that many—

"I'm off to a meeting and I've left a pile of items in your inbox."

"Great." Apparently that was the only word left in her vocabulary. "See you later," she called, as he swept into the elevator.

A date with RJ. Tonight. And she didn't even have to make the reservation! But she did still have to go through his correspondence and coordinate his schedule, just like any other day.

She felt as if she was stepping onto a board of chutes and ladders. Three steps forward and dinner with RJ leads up the tall ladder! What next? Would she roll a five and plunge to estrangement and unemployment at the bottom of a chute?

With no idea what kind of restaurant RJ would choose, Brooke decided to go smart-casual. She donned a floral patterned dress she'd never worn to work and a cute cashmere shrug she'd found in a boutique walking home from work one day. Her hair was shiny, her complexion clear for once and except for the heightened redness in her cheeks she looked pretty darn good!

Still, she jumped when the doorbell rang. She'd never given RJ her address, but no doubt he could just look in her personnel file. She drew in a breath as she walked across the living room to open the door.

"Hi." She felt yet another huge goofy grin spread across her face at the sight of RJ, several inches larger than life, as always, standing right there on her doorstep. "Won't you come in?" She'd spent at least an hour cleaning the place to within an inch of its life.

"Sure." He smiled, and stepped inside.

"Would you like a martini?" She knew he loved them.

"Why not?" RJ managed to look both classic and hip in a jacket that hung elegantly from his broad shoulders, and loose khakis. He often had the air of an old-time matinee idol, which perfectly matched his bold, aristocratic features and easy confidence. Right now she felt like his leading lady, since her dress had a vintage flair to it.

She mixed the martinis and poured them into long-stemmed glasses while RJ complimented her place.

"Thanks, I like it here." She'd lived in the two-bedroom condo near Colonial Lake for five years now and was proud of how she'd decorated it. A mix of timeless pieces and funky touches that reflected her personality. "I'm renting right now but I hope the owner will sell to me when the lease is up." *As long as I still have a job by then.* She smiled and handed him the drink. "Bottoms up."

RJ raised his glass. "I never know which end will be up lately." He took a sip, and nodded his head in approval. "You look gorgeous." His gaze lingered on her face, then drifted to her neck, and she became agonizingly conscious of the hint of cleavage her dress revealed.

"Thanks." She tried not to blush. "You don't look too bad, either." He'd obviously taken the time to go home and change after work, which touched her. She knew how often he headed out to dinner straight from the office.

"I clean up okay." He shot her a sultry look. "I'm glad to do something fun for a change. Lately I feel like I'm running from crisis to crisis, either in the company or in the family."

"Crisis-free here." She offered him a plate of tiny puff pastries she'd picked up on her way home. "Want something to nibble?"

"Why, sure." His eyes rested on her face for a second longer than was entirely polite. All the parts of her body that never knew how much they wanted to be nibbled by RJ started to hum and tingle. Then he took a pastry, put it in his mouth and chewed.

Brooke quickly swallowed one herself. She could see his gleaming black Porsche parked outside. She'd never ridden in it before as he used a more practical Audi sedan for work. She could imagine the neighbors whispering and peering through their miniblinds. "Where are we going for dinner?"

"A new place just off King Street. It's a grill, of

sorts, with a Low Country twist to it. A friend told me it's the best food he's eaten in ages."

"Sounds great, but isn't that kind of central? What if people see us together?" It probably wasn't the best idea for them to hang out right in the historic district. She'd assumed he'd pick somewhere discreet and out of the way.

"People see us together every day. Let them assume what they like."

Was he implying that this evening meant nothing so there was no need to worry if anyone saw?

The steady heat in his gaze suggested otherwise. If she didn't know better she'd suspect he could see right through her dress.

"I'd prefer to go somewhere more private." Her nerves jangled as she said it. He was her boss, after all, and not used to hearing her opinion on such things. "I'd hate for people to start talking."

"Let them talk. Everyone in Charleston is talking about the Kincaids right now and it hasn't killed us yet." His face darkened.

He must be thinking about his father's murder. Why was she bickering over restaurants when RJ was under so much pressure already? "All right, I'll stop worrying. We can always tell them we were testing it out as a place to hold a client party."

"Always thinking." He smiled and took another sip of his martini. "That's a damn good martini but I think we should get going. I made a reservation for eight and it's the hottest table in town right now."

Uh-oh. That meant there might be people he knew there. What if people started to gossip about them and things didn't work out? Her hands shook slightly as she put on her shrug and grabbed her purse. She was hoping for a promotion. What if people thought she was trying to sleep her way to the top? She was hardly from RJ's usual social circles. She swallowed hard. Still, it was too late to back out now. "I'm ready." She was heading out to dinner with her boss, for better or worse.

The reclined seats in his black Porsche felt every bit as decadent and inviting as she'd imagined. Excitement raced through her as RJ started the engine. She wouldn't be able to resist telling her mom about this. She'd be impressed for sure. Then again, maybe she was starting to think too much like her mom. She did not like RJ because he had a Porsche, or a large bank account—she liked him because of his intelligence and kindness.

And his washboard abs and fine backside.

"Why are you smiling?" His eyes twinkled when he glanced at her.

"I think the martini made me giddy."

"Excellent. I like you giddy."

He pulled into a parking space in the historic district, then opened her car door before she even had time to unbuckle her seat belt. He took her hand and helped her out, and she felt like royalty stepping onto King Street with RJ Kincaid. Which was funny because she'd been to restaurants here with him before—as part of a business party, of course. Now everything was different.

Her hand stayed inside RJ's, hot and aware, as they walked down a picturesque side street to a restaurant with a crisp green awning. The maître d' took them to their table on a veranda overlooking a tiny but perfect garden behind the building, where flowers climbed an old brick wall and water trickled in a lion's-head fountain. The table was set with a thick, starched tablecloth and heavy silverware, and a bright bouquet of daisies in a cut glass vase.

RJ pulled back her chair, again making her feel like a princess.

"A bottle of Moët, please," he said to the waiter.

Brooke's eyes widened. "What are we celebrating?"

"That life goes on." RJ leaned back in his chair. "And dammit, we're going to enjoy it no matter what happens."

"That's an admirable philosophy." Along with everyone else in Charleston, he must be wondering what could possibly happen next. His dad was dead and his mom was being held at the county jail under suspicion of murder. Bail had been denied as, with money and connections, she was considered a flight risk.

And there was something he didn't know.

Brooke had told the police she'd seen Mrs. Kincaid at the office that night. She hadn't mentioned this fact to RJ. In light of the arrest she wasn't sure he'd be happy she told the truth. Of course she knew Elizabeth Kincaid was innocent, but still... Guilt trickled uneasily up her spine. She really should tell him she'd seen his mom there. Just to clear the air.

"My dad would have wanted me to hold my head up and keep fighting." He watched as the waiter poured two tall glasses of sparkling champagne. "And that's what I intend to do. I spent all afternoon trying to get the D.A.'s office to agree to set bail for Mom, but they've refused. And I talked Apex International down from the ledge in between phone calls to the D.A."

"The toy importer?"

"Yup. Getting ready to jump ship to one of our competitors. I convinced them to stick with us. Told them the Kincaid Group is the most efficient, well-run, cost-effective shipper on the east coast and we intend to stay that way." He raised his glass and clinked it gently against hers. "Thanks for brightening a dark day."

His honest expression, weary but still brave and strong, touched something deep inside her. "I'm happy to help in any way I can." That sounded odd. A bit too businesslike, maybe. But it was hard to step out of her familiar role and embrace this new one, especially when she had no idea what role she'd be in tomorrow. *You know I'd do anything for you.* She managed not to say it, though she suspected he knew.

"You're helping already." That little flame of desire hovered in his pupils and sent a shiver through her. "Your loyalty means a lot to me. You've proved I can count on you in a crisis. I don't know what I would have done without you in the last few weeks."

His deep voice echoed inside her. Did she really mean that much to him? Her heart fluttered alarmingly. "I'm glad."

Further words failed her and she distracted herself by looking down at the menu, which had an array of elegant yet folksy-sounding local dishes. After some hemming and hawing, RJ chose roast pork shoulder with mustard barbeque sauce and sautéed greens. She chose a shrimp dish with a side of grits and an arugula salad.

"It occurs to me that I don't know too much about you, Brooke Nichols." RJ raised a brow. "I know you live in Charleston, but other than that you're a bit of an enigma. You don't talk about yourself much."

She inhaled slightly. "There isn't much to know." Did he really want to learn that her college quarterback father had resisted all her teenage mother's attempts to trap him into marriage, and how she'd grown up with a succession of stepfathers? "I was born in Greenville, and I went to high school in Columbia. Mom and I moved here after I graduated and we both adore it."

"Does your mom live with you?"

"No, she lives in the 'burbs." With her latest boyfriend. "I enjoy having my own place."

"Do you? I find I'm getting tired of living alone. I miss Mom's cooking." He smiled, then a shadow of pain passed over his features.

A jolt of guilt tightened her stomach. Was her police interview the reason Elizabeth Kincaid had been arrested? She really should tell RJ about that right now. *Did you know I told the police I saw your mom at the scene of the crime?* How did you say something like that without sounding accusatory? "I'm sure they'll let her out soon. They have to know she's innocent. She's the sweetest lady I've ever met." She wasn't exaggerating. And now she knew what Elizabeth Kincaid had put up with over the years. She must have suspected her husband was cheating, at least, even if she hadn't known about his second family. "I wish we could help them find the real killer."

"Me, too. Mom's always been the linchpin of the family. I'm trying to hold it together for everyone but we're all tense and anxious."

Her heart swelled. "I envy your large family. It must

be reassuring to have siblings you can turn to as well as your parents."

"Or fight with." He grinned. "I think we probably argue as much as we get along. Maybe not so much these days, but when we were kids..." He shook his head.

"I never had anybody to fight with, and I'm not sure that's a good thing. Sibling spats must teach you how to negotiate with people."

He laughed. "Are you saying I honed my business bargaining skills over the Hot Wheels set I shared with Matt?"

"Quite possibly." She sipped her champagne, a smile spreading across her lips. RJ was visibly relaxing, his features softening and the lines of worry leaving his face. "Whatever you did as children has made you close as adults. I don't think I've ever seen a family spend so much time together."

RJ sighed. "I really thought we were the perfect family, but now the entire world knows that was just an illusion."

"No family is perfect. Yours is still close-knit and loving, even after everything that's happened."

The waiter brought their appetizers, fried calamari with a green tomato salsa.

"We'll get through this. I need to focus on what makes us stronger, not what's threatening to tear us apart. And somehow you've managed to deflect the conversation off yourself again." He raised a brow. "You're a mysterious character, Brooke. What do you do when you're peacefully alone in your private palace?"

She shrugged. It would have been nice to be able

to chatter gaily about flamenco dancing sessions and cocktail parties, but she wasn't one to embroider the truth. She had friends over once or twice a month, but mostly she valued the peace and quiet of her sanctuary after a long day at work. "I read a lot." She paused to nibble a crispy piece of calamari. "Not very exciting, is it?"

"I guess that depends on how good a book you're reading." His blue gaze rested on her face, and she warmed under it. "Sometimes I think I should make more time for quiet pastimes like reading. Might improve my mind."

She laughed. "I can't see you sitting still long enough to read a book."

"Maybe that's something I need to work on." He hadn't touched his food. If anything he seemed transfixed by her, unable to take his eyes off her face. Brooke felt her breathing grow shallow under his intense stare. "I used to go out to our hunting cabin at least once a month with my dad. We'd mellow out and recharge our batteries together. I haven't been there since he died."

"Can you still go visit it?"

"It's mine now. He left it to me in his will." A shadow passed over his face. The same will that left almost half the company to Jack Sinclair. "It's been sitting empty since he died."

"Why don't you go there?"

He shrugged. "I never went there without Dad. I can't imagine going alone and I can't think of anyone I'd want to go with." His expression changed and his eyes widened slightly. "You. You could come with me."

"Oh, I don't think so." She shifted in her chair. Their

first date wasn't even over yet and he was inviting her on an overnight trip? She knew his family never went there just for the day. It was probably a long drive. She'd likely be expected to share a bed with him and so far they'd only kissed once. Already her heart pounded with a mix of excitement and sheer terror.

RJ's face brightened. "We'll go this weekend. Just you and me. We'll get Frankie Deleon's to pack us some gourmet meals and we'll spend a weekend in peace."

"I don't know anything about hunting." The idea of killing things made her cringe.

"Don't worry, we don't have to really hunt. Dad and I mostly just walked around in the mountains carrying the guns as an excuse. It's so peaceful up there it seems a crime to pierce the air with a shot."

She smiled. "That's a funny image. So there aren't racks of antlers on the living room wall?"

"There's one set but we bought it at an antiques auction." His eyes twinkled. "We call him Uncle Dave. We did sometimes go fishing and eat the fish, though. Fishing was the only time I ever saw Dad sit still for more than a few minutes."

"I used to fish with my friend June's family years ago. They'd take a camper to a lake and stay there for a week every summer. I caught a huge rainbow trout once."

"Excellent. Now we know what we're doing this weekend." He rubbed his hands together with enthusiasm. "Nice to have something to look forward to as this promises to be a long week."

Brooke didn't know what to say. He'd already planned her weekend without even waiting for a response. Yes, he was her boss, but going fishing on the weekends was not part of her job description. She should be mad at his arrogance.

On the other hand, a weekend in the mountains with RJ… What girl would say no to that?

Her. "I don't think I should come. I'm sure you have other friends you could invite." Her gut was telling her to slow this whole train ride before it went off the tracks. "I have…things to do here at home."

"Are you afraid I'll take advantage of you, out there in the lonesome woods?" He tilted his head and lifted a brow.

"Yes." Her blood sizzled at the prospect.

"You're absolutely right, of course."

"I think it's a bit premature."

"Of course, we've only known each other five years." A dimple appeared in his left cheek, emphasizing his high cheekbones.

"You know what I mean."

"Sure. One amazing kiss is not enough to plan an entire weekend around."

She shrugged. "Something like that."

"How many kisses? Two, three?" He looked impatiently at the expanse of tablecloth between them. Humor twinkled in his eyes.

"Probably somewhere around five." She fought to keep a smile from her mouth.

"Five years and five kisses." He looked thoughtful. "Let's see what we can do before the night is out."

The handsome waiter whisked their appetizer plates away and settled their mains in front of them while the sommelier poured two glasses of white wine. She'd barely made a dent in her champagne. Maybe that was her problem. She needed to drink a bit more to take the edge off her inhibitions. The whiskey had certainly done wonders for RJ yesterday. On the other hand, the prospect of four more kisses before the evening ended made her light-headed.

She could see the glow of impending victory in RJ's eyes. She'd become familiar with that look in meetings right when he knew he'd clinched a big deal. RJ hated to lose, and sometimes went after quite small clients just for the satisfaction of beating the competition.

Apparently she was to be his next conquest. Her blood pressure ratcheted up a notch. RJ in motion was hard to stop. "Can you really get away for the weekend with everything that's going on right now?"

RJ raised a dark brow. "That's exactly why I need to get away." He reached out and touched her fingers gently where they sat at the base of her glass. A tiny shiver of arousal ran through her. "And you're just the distraction I need."

His voice was husky, thick with the arousal that weighted the air between them. Did he expect her to go home with him tonight? Just what had she gotten herself into here? Him calling her a "distraction" did not entirely bode well for a lifelong commitment.

Then again, she was getting way ahead of herself. And already her lips tingled in anticipation of the second kiss he'd promised. She tried to distract them with a piece of shrimp, but the sauce proved surprisingly spicy and only made things worse. "I suppose some fresh air won't do either of us any harm." That sounded lame. She should probably be making suggestive and witty comments. Soon enough RJ would realize he'd made a terrible mistake thinking she was an attractive and desirable woman.

If he even did think that. Maybe it was more of an "any port in the storm" thing. Even your assistant started to look good when your entire world was falling apart.

"What *are* you thinking about?" RJ peered into her eyes, mischief sparkling in his own blue depths.

"Just wondering where this evening is heading." The truth seemed as good a response as any other.

RJ's mouth broadened into a sensual smile. "Somewhere beautiful."

It was dark when they parked near Waterfront Park and strolled along the promenade looking out at the lights reflected on the dark water. They were dangerously close to RJ's apartment, or at least she suspected so, but he'd shown no signs of trying to take her home. He hadn't even tried to kiss her.

Her skin craved his touch and each time she hoped for it and didn't get it, the longing only grew more bone-deep. Five years of suppressed yearning were unleashed by one kiss, and if she didn't get another kiss soon she might just burst into flame.

Moonlight mingled with the streetlights to illuminate RJ's dramatic features. "So your mom is your only real family?"

"Since my Gran died five years ago, yes." RJ had been plumbing her for information all evening. Not in an unkind way. He seemed genuinely curious.

"Did you ever want siblings?"

"All the time," she admitted. "When I was little I wished for a sister to share my dolls with. Then when I was a teenager I wished I had a brother to bring home handsome friends."

He chuckled. "My sisters weren't shy about asking me to do just that. But I bet you managed fine, anyway."

He caressed her with another one of those lingering glances that made her feel like a supermodel. No need for him to know her last date had been nearly a year ago. Since her best friend got married she hadn't been out much at night and she knew better than to have an affair with someone at the office.

Until now…

He stepped toward her and slid his arms around her hips. Her breasts stirred inside her dress as he pulled her close. Her lips parted and her hands rose to the soft wool of his jacket. She ached for his kiss, a long, deep ache that rose inside her and pulled her closer into his embrace. When his lips finally met hers sensation sparkled through her. All day she'd dreamed of this moment, craved and hoped for it, despite all her misgivings. RJ's arms around her made her feel safe, protected and adored. He kissed with exquisite gentleness, touching her lips gently then pulling back, letting the very tip of his tongue touch hers, teasing and tasting her until she was in a frenzy of arousal. It took all her strength not to writhe against him in full view of the other people enjoying the breezy moonlit night.

"Yes, it's a good idea." RJ's words surprised her. "Us kissing." They'd barely pulled apart and she hadn't even had time for doubts to creep back into her consciousness. No doubt he was trying to preempt them.

"Certainly feels like one." A silly smile plastered itself across her face. A sense of euphoria suffused her entire body, and she'd only had two glasses of wine so she couldn't even blame the alcohol.

She was high on RJ.

His lips touched hers again, and again her synapses lit up like a Christmas tree. She'd never experienced such a sharp physical reaction to a simple kiss. It was a full-body experience. By the time he pulled gently back she was sure she'd broken out in a sweat.

Already her lips itched to meet his again. But if she gave him all five kisses, was she agreeing to the weekend away? "I really should get home now."

"No way." His hands held her steady. "Five years, five kisses."

"There's nothing about kisses in my employment contract." She attempted to look fierce.

"There wouldn't be, since we don't use an employment contract." That naughty dimple appeared again as he lowered his lips to hers. Brooke's lips parted instinctively, and a tantalizing tip of his tongue probed her mouth, sending a shiver of suggestion down her spine. Her knees wobbled and she was forced to hold him tighter. With her pressed against his hard chest, kiss number three was broken only by a quiet whisper. "Brooke, why did we wait so long?"

She didn't answer. Boring explanations about her long-term career prospects had no place in this electric moment. Kiss number four crept up on them and her eyes shut tight as sensation swept through her. RJ's hard chest felt like a safe foundation to lean on, so she let the world drift away and lost herself in his kiss. An hour could have passed before their lips finally pulled apart, she had no idea.

The streetlights, even the reflected glow from the

water, seemed painfully bright when she opened her eyes.

"I expect you're wondering if I'm going to ask you back to my apartment." RJ looked down at her, arms still wrapped around her, holding her close.

The thought did cross my mind. She kept her mouth closed, though. She still had no idea what she'd reply if he did ask.

"I'm not."

A tiny frisson of disappointment cascaded through her. Had this evening led him to decide he was no longer interested in her? Maybe he just liked talking to her and didn't want to take it further. Perhaps those kisses that lit her whole body on fire had simply been a series of tests that she'd failed.

"I have the utmost respect for you, Brooke." His expression was serious.

Her heart sank further. Was this the "you're too valuable an employee for me to fool around with" speech?

"I know you're a lady and would be offended if I asked you in on our first date." He moved his hands until they were over hers. "And I'm still enough of a gentleman to resist the temptation."

His fingers wove into hers and the full force of that temptation rushed through her. He was taking it slow because he respected her. Somehow that truly touched her.

He leaned in until she could inhale his enticing male scent. "But I'm not letting you go without one last kiss."

Relief swept through her as their lips pressed together. He wasn't rejecting her. She held him tight and kissed him back with passion.

"And I'm already anticipating the pleasure of an entire weekend with you, so asking for tonight as well would be greedy."

Misgivings still crept in her veins. An entire weekend was a long time. If things got out of hand there would be no turning back. Though likely it was already too late to return to their normal workaday existence. "What should I bring?" Would she need waders, or an evening gown? Or both?

"Just yourself. The house is fully stocked for entertaining guests so there's loads of extra gear there."

"Will anyone else be there?" What if other Kincaid siblings were around to witness her liaison with RJ? She cringed at the thought of them laughing behind her back, or exchanging shocked whispers.

"I certainly hope not." RJ pressed a quick kiss to her lips. "Since the house is mine now and I haven't invited anyone but you we should have the whole two hundred acres to ourselves."

Two hundred acres. It must be in the middle of nowhere. Of course that was probably the point with hunting cabins. Less chance of shooting one of the neighbors. She and RJ would have more than enough privacy to do anything they liked.

Which reminded her she was arm in arm with him in a popular spot in downtown Charleston. Did she really want coworkers or his family to see them kissing? They might think she was trying to sleep her way to a promotion. Or even take advantage of him when he was under stress. "I think it's time for me to go home. I have to work tomorrow—and so do you in case you've forgotten." It was nearly eleven last time she'd checked.

"I don't have to worry. My capable assistant handles everything for me while I take long lunches."

Brooke made a mock gasp. "I'll have to schedule some of those investor conferences you so look forward to. Perhaps some early breakfast meetings."

"Now you're scaring me. I'll do my best to roll in after a late breakfast."

His cocky attitude didn't annoy her. In fact she was proud he could count on her to keep his work life on track. He looked so relaxed and happy right now you'd never guess his family was in turmoil. Maybe she could take some credit for that, as well.

A warm sense of satisfaction bloomed inside her, along with the delicious arousal RJ had stirred. If things went well this weekend, who knew what the future might hold?

Three

"You're going to spend the weekend in the woods with *your boss?*" Her friend Evie had been speechless for a few seconds. Now apparently she'd recovered.

Brooke moved the phone back closer to her ear again. "He's quite different than I thought. Much more sensitive."

"I don't care how sensitive he is. What will happen when he gets bored with you?"

"Ouch." Brooke walked across her apartment. "Am I that dull? You've been friends with me for nearly eight years."

"You know what I mean. Most men, especially in his position, just want to fool around and have fun, and after a few dates they're ready for someone new. Didn't you tell me yourself that he's a bit of a Casanova?"

"Sure, he used to date a lot, but this big family scandal has made him more serious." He hadn't been going out much lately. At least not that she knew of.

"So he's turned into the white picket fence type and is looking for a nice, quiet girl to settle down with."

"Maybe he is."

"You could be right, but what if he isn't? You've put five years into the company. Didn't you say something about a management position?"

"I applied to be the events coordinator but I didn't get it." Yes, it smarted a little, especially since the woman they'd hired from outside was more than a bit flaky. "I just have to keep trying."

"And you think an affair with your boss will help?"

"It's not an affair yet. All we've done is kiss."

"After a weekend in the woods it will be an affair. Do you genuinely believe he'll decide you're the girl of his dreams and ask you to marry him?"

Brooke took in a breath. "Is it a crime to dream? You're married."

"To the guy in the next cubicle, not the one at the head of the boardroom table. I care about you, Brooke, and I know how much your job at Kincaid means to you. It really is a place where you could take your career to the next level and I don't want to see you throw that away for a quick sympathy fling."

"I can always find a job somewhere else."

"In this economy? I'm being very careful with the job I have as there's not a lot out there."

"You're so supportive." Her joy had deflated. One minute she'd been swanning around the air castles of her mind as Mrs. RJ Kincaid. Then the castle went poof and she was now single again and jobless, too. "Maybe I want to have some fun."

Evie sighed. "I miss our nights out together. I know being married is no reason to stay in every night, but we have our hands full with this renovation project right now and—"

Brooke laughed. "I wasn't trying to guilt trip you into a night on the town with me. I know it sounds crazy but the roller coaster has already left the station. I can't go back to before the kiss, so I might as well enjoy the ride and hope for the best."

"My knuckles are turning white just thinking about it. And I want to hear *all* the details on Monday."

RJ left his keys and wallet on the tray and walked through the security machines at the detention center. His entire body reacted to the oppressive atmosphere of the building. A place where hardened criminals were locked up awaiting trial, and where his kind and gentle mother was forced to suffer their company.

A silent guard led him to a private interview room. His lawyer had apparently gone to great trouble to arrange a face-to-face meeting with his mom, otherwise he could only speak to her from the lobby over a video link. The guard opened the door to a small room with a metal desk and two chairs.

She looked tiny, sitting alone at the desk, dressed in the regulation jumpsuit. He walked toward her, unable to govern his features into any kind of polite greeting. "Mom." He took her in his arms and held her tight. She seemed so frail and helpless, not at all the steel magnolia he'd always proudly bragged about.

"No contact." He'd forgotten the no touching rule, and the gruff voice behind him reminded him. With great reluctance he pulled back his arms.

"I won't do it again." He turned to the guard. "Can we be alone for a few minutes?"

"I'll be standing right here, watching." The tall, older man gestured to a square of window in the door, then slipped outside.

His mom's face was pale and drawn, with tiny blue shadows under her expressive eyes. Her trademark auburn hair was slicked back in a way that only made her look more gaunt and slender.

"I'm trying everything to get you out of here."

"I know." The barest hint of a smile lit her eyes. "My lawyer says you won't even let him sleep."

"He can sleep later, once you're free. I'm going to see the D.A. again this afternoon, before I go away for the weekend."

"Are you going to the lodge?" Her eyes brightened. He nodded. "I wondered how long it would take before you went there again. I know how much you love it up in the mountains. Who's going with you?"

"Brooke." Why not tell the truth? Anticipation rose in his veins like sap in the spring. He couldn't wait to be alone with Brooke on that peaceful mountainside. He could already picture sunbeams picking out gold in her hair, and those soft green eyes gazing at the majestic views. She'd love it there. He knew she would.

"Your assistant?" His mom's shocked response drew him from his reverie. Her pale eyebrows lacked their usual flourish of pencil, but he still saw them rise.

"Yes. She and I… She's been a great help to me lately." His brain filled almost to bursting with a desire to tell his mom all about his newfound relationship with Brooke. Brooke was sweet and kind as well as beautiful and he was sure his mom would love her.

Still, he could tell his mom was shocked by the idea of him dating his own assistant and somehow it seemed premature, so he held his tongue.

She nodded. "She seems a bright girl, and very pretty. I hope you have a lovely time. You certainly deserve a break and some fresh air. I know how hard you've been working."

"Thanks, Mom." His chest tightened. How sweet she was to wish him a good weekend when she'd be stuck in here. Anger and frustration raged inside him again. "Why are they holding you? No one will explain. I can't understand why they won't let you out on bail. I had a hell of a time even coming to see you in person."

His mom glanced around the room. "Sit down, will you." She gestured politely as if inviting him to take up residence in one of her beautifully upholstered Liberty print chairs at home, not a scarred metal folding chair.

RJ sat.

She leaned toward him. "They know I was in the office on the night…the night your dad was shot." Her voice faded on the last word and he saw pain flash in her eyes.

"You were there?" He kept his voice as hushed as possible.

"I was." Her lips closed tightly for a second, draining of blood. "I brought him a plate of food as he'd said he'd be home late."

RJ frowned. "They didn't say any food had been found."

She shook her head. "He didn't want it so I took it home with me." She let out a sigh, which rippled through her body as a visible shiver. "I know it seems odd, me bringing him dinner. I only did it that night as I was worried your dad had been so distant, like he was troubled by something. I'd been short with him the night before and I wanted to show him I cared."

"Dad knew you cared about him." RJ's heart filled with red-hot rage that his dad had caused her so much pain by carrying on with another woman. "If anything, he didn't deserve you."

Her eyes filled with tears, but she managed to blink them back. "I do miss your father, even after all that's happened."

"Of course you do." He took her hands in his. They were cold and bony, and he chafed them lightly, trying to warm them. "But you bringing dinner doesn't make you a murderer."

"It makes me a murder suspect."

RJ frowned. Something was seriously off here. "But how did the police know you were there?" The front desk didn't bother logging family members or employees, who were allowed to come and go as they pleased.

"Someone saw me."

"Who?" What kind of person would finger his mom at the crime scene?

She hesitated. Looked away. "Does it really matter? I don't even remember if anyone saw me. As I said, I was there."

"The accusations still don't make sense. You have no motivation to kill Dad. For one thing, you were as much in the dark as the rest of us about Angela and her sons." The words soured in his mouth. "I wish to God none of us had ever found out."

She pulled her hands back and placed them in her lap. "I have a confession to make, RJ."

RJ's eyes widened. "What?" Was she going to admit to killing his dad? His stomach roiled.

"I did know about Angela." Her eyes were dry, her expression composed. "I'd known for some years. Ever since I found an earlier version of Reginald's will in his desk while looking for a calculator."

RJ swallowed. So his suspicion was correct. "Why didn't you say anything?"

"Your father and I had words, but he convinced me to stay with him for the sake of the family. The reputation, the company, you know how important all that was to him." She smoothed back her hair. "And to me."

He blinked, unable to process this. "So you were sitting there with us at family dinners, week after week, and you never breathed a word to anyone?"

Her head hung slightly, and lines of pain formed around her eyes. "Your father and I were married for a very long time. There was a lot of history there. Maybe too much to throw away for an affair that began so long ago."

"But that was still continuing, unless I understand wrong."

He watched his mom's throat move as she swallowed. "You're not wrong. Reginald loved Angela." It took visible effort for her gaze to meet his, and he fought the urge to take her in his arms again. Her rigid posture told him to keep his distance. "He loved me, too." A wry smile tugged at her lips. "He was a man with a lot of love to give."

"That's one way of looking at it, though I'd like the opportunity to give him a piece of my mind." He realized his hands were clenched into fists, and he released them. "I know you didn't kill him." He had to say it, because he had thought it for that split second after she announced a confession, and he needed to clear the air.

"Of course I didn't, but the police and the courts don't know that, and I don't have an alibi for the time of the murder."

"We need to find out who really did it. Do you have any suspicions?"

She shook her head. "Trust me, if I had even the slightest inkling, I'd tell everyone I know."

RJ glanced around the grim room. "This place is a nightmare." He remembered the bag he'd brought with him. "I brought you some books. Flannery O'Connor, William Faulkner. Lily said you'd want something more cheery, but I wasn't so sure. They put them through the metal detector downstairs. Apparently razor-sharp wit doesn't show up on the screen."

She smiled, and peered into the offered paper bag. "RJ, you're so thoughtful. And you're right, I feel like reading about experiences darker than my own." She sighed. "Hopefully I won't have time to read them all."

"Not if I can help it."

"I've never flown in a small plane." Brooke's hands trembled as she buckled the seat belt in the Kincaid jet. "Couldn't we drive there?" Her wide green eyes implored him.

A protective instinct surged inside RJ and he took hold of her hand. "It's almost 150 miles away, near Gatlinburg, Tennessee. We'll be fine." Strange to see ever-capable Brooke looking worried. He squeezed her trembling fingers gently to reassure her. "At least we have a professional pilot today. My dad used to fly it himself sometimes and while he claimed military flying experience, I never saw any kind of license."

"Scary!"

"Tell me about it. I even toyed with getting a license myself so I'd be able to take over in an emergency. One time we got caught in a wind shear coming out of the mountains, but Dad handled it like a pro." His chest tightened as a wave of sadness swept through him. He still couldn't believe that he'd never see his dad again. Never hear his chesty laugh or another tall tale about his days in Special Ops.

"You're not making me feel better."

"We'll be fine." He lifted his arm and placed it around her shoulder. Her soft floral scent filled his nostrils. Soon they'd be alone together in the mountains. The fresh air would lift the cares off both of their shoulders. He couldn't wait to hear her infectious laugh echo off the wooded hillsides, or see the morning sun sparkle in her lovely eyes. And then there would be the nights… He'd instructed the caretaker to put the best fresh linen on the beds—he planned to offer her one for herself, then tempt her out of it. The prospect of Brooke's lush body writhing under those sheets made his pulse quicken.

Yes, she was his assistant. Doubts did force their way to the forefront of his consciousness from time to time. Mixing business and pleasure was always risky, and in a family business it could be downright explosive. His father had warned all of them to keep their personal affairs out of the office and RJ had never had an affair with an employee before, despite considerable temptation over the years. Funnily enough he'd never seen Brooke in that way until their whiskey-flavored kiss in his office. She'd been his right-hand woman, his trusted friend, his rock—but their kiss had opened up a new world of possibilities.

Now he knew his assistant was a sensual woman, with passion flickering behind the jade of her eyes and excited breaths quickening in her lovely chest when he looked at her, the temptation was irresistible. He'd never have dreamed anything could take his mind off the hailstorm of disaster raining down on the Kincaid family over the last few months, but when he was with Brooke, all his burdens seemed lighter. It was such a relief to be with someone whom he could totally trust.

He heard Brooke's breath catch as the plane lifted off the runway, but she soon relaxed as they rose high over the Charleston suburbs, heading toward the sunset and the distant shadow of the mountains. If only they could fly away from all his troubles and worries. Those were hitchhiking along, but with Brooke by his side they'd stay in check.

"How's your mom doing?" Brooke's soft question revealed her natural empathy.

"She's hanging in there. She's a brave woman and she doesn't want us to worry. I visited her this afternoon and took her some books she wanted. I told her we're doing everything we can to get her out. The police have been pretty closemouthed so I hired a private investigator to work full-time on the case, and he's going to work with Nikki Thomas, our own corporate investigator. The lawyers are still trying to negotiate bail. They keep promising she'll be released but it gets shot down at the last moment. Apparently someone saw her in the office that night. Hey, are you okay?"

Brooke's face had turned so pale, even her lips lost color. "Sure, just a little queasy. I'll be okay."

He squeezed her hand. It was easy to dismiss your own problems, but you couldn't always help the ones you cared about. Lately that made him feel powerless, an unfamiliar experience he hated. At least he could show Brooke a glorious and relaxing weekend in the country. She deserved the best of everything and he intended to give it to her.

Brooke gripped his hand tightly during their descent into the airport at Gatlinburg, then exhaled with relief as the plane taxied to a halt.

"See? You survived."

"Only just. And my nails have probably left permanent scars on your hand."

"I'll wear them with pride."

RJ was pleased to see the caretaker had dropped the familiar black Suburban off at the airport then discreetly disappeared. The first sign that his plans were going smoothly. He'd told the caretaker he didn't need any staff on hand, as he suspected Brooke might be spooked by the presence of other people. Much better that they enjoy peace and privacy.

A now-familiar pang of grief hit him as he climbed behind the wheel. His dad usually drove, maintaining the familiar patterns of father-and-son even though RJ had been driving for nearly twenty years. "Dad loved it up here. He always said the whole world fell away if you got high enough up into the mountains."

"It's beautiful. The light is different here." That light illuminated Brooke's hair and her delicate profile as she looked out the window. For a split second he longed to press his lips to hers and lose himself in a kiss. Instead he started the engine.

"Dad wrote me a letter when he made his will." He frowned. He'd never spoken to anyone else about it. "Said he wasn't sure how much longer he'd live and he wanted to make sure the lodge would be mine."

"Oh." Brooke turned sharply, shock written on her face. "Sounds like he almost knew he was going to die."

"He never said a word to anyone." He shook his head. "His lawyers told me he redrew his will every few years, so they didn't think much of it. He included letters each time. But when he died there was one for everyone in the family…except my mom."

"Did he leave any hints of who he suspected?"

"That is odd. Nothing I could figure out. He does mention his other family that none of us knew about. Well, except Mom."

"Your mom knew about his other woman and her children?"

RJ swallowed. "Apparently so. She didn't say anything to us. She learned about them while he was writing his will. She found a copy in his desk." It was good to get that awkward truth off his chest. He knew he could trust Brooke not to tell anyone. "She didn't want any of us to know."

"Is that why police think she has motive?"

"I suppose they think she wanted revenge." He heard Brooke's intake of breath. Did she think it was possible that his mom could wield a gun against her husband of nearly four decades? "You do know she's innocent."

"Yes, of course." The color had fled her cheeks again. "It's just a shame she had to find out that way."

Brooke seemed distracted, staring hard out the window, not even noticing the bait and tackle shop and the quaint country inn he'd intended to show her.

"I brought Dad's letter with me because he mentions something in the lodge." He paused while a big truck crossed at the intersection ahead. "Something else he wanted me to have."

"An object?"

"I don't know. It's rather mysterious. He said to look in the third drawer down, but he didn't say what piece of furniture."

"Hmm. I guess you'll just have to open every third drawer down in the house, and hope for the best."

He didn't mention the other things his dad had said in the letter. For now those were between Reginald Kincaid, Sr., and his namesake, and maybe it was better that no one else knew about them.

Brooke was lost for words when they pulled up at the lodge. Then again, what had she expected, a shack with an outside toilet? This was a Kincaid residence. The vast log home rose up out of the surrounding woodlands, high gables braced with chiseled beams and walls of windows reflecting the sunset. RJ strode up the steps and unlocked the impressive double doors, then ushered her inside.

Golden sunlight illuminated the foyer from all directions. RJ put down their bags then walked through a door in the far wall. "Dad named it Great Oak Lodge. Come see why we built the house here."

Brooke followed him into another grand room, decorated in an updated, minimalist interpretation of hunting-lodge chic: pale sofas with muted plaid accents, a painting of a stag and an impressive stone fireplace. The last rays of sunlight blazing in through a wall of windows largely obscured the view, until RJ opened a pair of patio doors and she saw an endless vista of tree-cloaked hills.

She walked out and stood beside him. There were no signs of civilization at all, just peaks and valleys filled with more trees. "It feels like we're on top of the world."

"Maybe we are." He stepped behind her and slid his arms around her waist. Her belly shimmered with arousal. They hadn't kissed since their date two nights ago, and on the plane she'd been too nervous to think much about kissing. Or any of the things that might follow.

RJ bent his head and pressed his lips to her neck. "You smell sensational." Excitement trickled through her, peppered with anxiety about where this was all going. Now his hot breath warmed her ear, making her shiver with anticipation.

"Shouldn't we put our bags away?" She could hardly believe that was her voice interrupting the sensual moment.

RJ chuckled. "Trying to delay the inevitable?"

"Just being practical. That's why you hired me." Ouch. Why did she have to remind him—and herself—that she was his employee?

"Let's leave the office at the office." RJ still held her tight in his embrace, and his mouth had moved barely an inch from her skin. "Do you think any of those trees care about memos and meetings and deadlines? It's a whole different world up here. Breathe in some fresh mountain air."

"I think I am." Surely if she wasn't she'd have passed out by now. Which was a distinct possibility the way RJ was tantalizing her earlobe with his tongue and teeth.

"Mountain air is restorative. Draw it all the way to the bottom of your lungs."

She drew a breath deep down into her belly the way she'd learned in yoga class. Evening cool, scented with pine and fresh soil, the rich air filled her lungs, and she exhaled with gusto. "That does feel good."

"Standing up here restores perspective. Out here it seems like time doesn't exist—the sun rises and sets and everything stays the same except the slow change of the seasons."

"RJ, you're turning out to have more dimensions than I expected."

"And you've known me five years already. Just shows how important it is to step out of context. Now kiss me."

Before she could protest he spun her around and pressed his lips firmly to hers. Her eyes slid shut and her hands rose to his shoulders. The kiss was delicious, golden and heady as the sunset warming their skin. The slight stubble on RJ's chin tickled her and she felt his eyelashes flutter against her cheeks as he deepened the kiss.

She hugged him, enjoying the closeness she'd craved, letting go of her worries and losing herself in the powerful sensation of his strong arms around her waist, holding her tight.

When they finally pulled apart, by only a feather's depth, his eyes sparkled and she knew hers did, too.

Happiness swelled in her chest and the moment felt so perfect.

"You're a very beautiful woman, Brooke. The sunset suits you."

"Maybe I should wear it every day."

"Most definitely. And I have a feeling that sunrise will become you, as well."

"I guess we'll have to get up early and find out." A tiny blade of anxiety poked her stomach. By morning they would have slept together.

Or would they?

After they disentangled themselves from each other's arms, RJ took her to a bedroom with panoramic views and invited her to unpack. Then he disappeared. Maybe they weren't going to sleep together at all. The closet was empty, except for a few hangers and a plain white terry bathrobe. The room had an adjoining bath, with freshly unwrapped soap and tiny bottles of expensive Kiehl's shampoo and conditioner. The rustic yet elegant bentwood bed was covered with a thick, soft duvet and the whole room was decorated in neutral colors that complemented the jaw-dropping view out the window. It was like being in a very high-end hotel.

Brooke hung her few items in the cavernous closet, then changed out of her work suit into her favorite jeans and a green shirt that highlighted her eyes. The carpets were soft pure wool, so she left her feet bare to better enjoy them and show off her rather daring jade-green toenails.

She peered out into the hallway. She followed the sound of whistling and found RJ in a similarly spacious bedroom, with a large bed made of rustic planks, checking his phone. "Settled in?"

"Perfectly." There was his bag, half-unpacked, on top of a pine chest of drawers. So they were sleeping in separate bedrooms. She should be relieved, but instead she felt disappointed. Maybe she was hoping for a whirlwind romance and he just planned to cast some flies and kick back in the sunshine.

"I've never seen you in jeans before." His eyes roamed down her legs, heating her skin through the denim. "Clearly, I've been missing out."

"I've never seen you in jeans before, either." She smiled, glancing at the pair peeking out of his duffel bag.

"Mine don't hug me quite the way yours do." A dimple played in his cheek.

"Shame." A sudden vision of RJ's body flashed in her mind. Even in his suit—the jacket hung over a corner of the wardrobe door and his sleeves were rolled up—you could see he was built and muscular. He played a lot of tennis and squash and sailed competitively. No doubt his muscles were bronzed by all that time in the sun. Hopefully soon she'd get to compare her imagination to reality.

If that was really a good idea.

"Are you hungry?" RJ's expression suggested he wanted for something entirely different than food.

"I am. All that shaking with terror on the flight built up an appetite."

"Good, because I'm making dinner."

Her eyes widened. RJ Kincaid in front of a stove?

"Don't look so shocked. You should know by now that I'm a man of many talents."

"I'm impressed."

"One of my talents is delegating to skilled professionals." He strode out of the room, leaving his phone on the bed. "Frankie Deleon owns the best restaurant in town and this afternoon I had the fridge stocked with provisions." She followed him into a bright kitchen with gleaming professional quality appliances. He pulled open one door on the fridge. The inside revealed a collection of smart earthenware dishes, each labeled with a Post-it note. "Let's see, jambalaya, baby back ribs, black-eyed peas and greens—hey, those need actual cooking. Poached salmon, sesame noodles." He moved a dish aside to reach behind it. "Macaroni and cheese, rice salad, green salad, beet and goat cheese salad… Where do you want to start?"

Brooke's mouth was already watering. She could get used to this Kincaid lifestyle. "It all sounds sensational. What are you in the mood for?"

His blue gaze settled on her face and she read her answer loud and clear. A smile crept across her mouth as her nipples tightened under her green shirt.

"You decide."

A challenge. She knew RJ liked people who could think on their feet and make executive decisions. "Ribs with sesame noodles and green salad."

"I like." RJ pulled the containers from the shelves and placed them on a butcher-block island large enough to have its own sink. Brooke turned on one of the stainless steel ovens, and RJ pulled some fine china dishes from one of the cabinets. They picked a chilled white wine to sip while waiting for the ribs to bake.

"Did you check the drawers yet?"

RJ looked up from the bottle opener. "What drawers?"

"The one mentioned in your dad's letter." Maybe

that was too personal. He probably wanted to search for the item alone.

He looked back down at the bottle. "I'm not sure I'm ready yet. I still hardly believe he's gone."

"I can't imagine what a shock it must have been."

"I keep expecting him to walk around the corner and say it was all an elaborate hoax." He gestured toward a wing-backed red chair in the great room adjoining the kitchen. "That was his favorite chair. I feel like he's going to get up out of it and rib me for not catching any fish yet this year."

The cork popped out with force, almost making Brooke jump. "I know he's proud of you for how you're handling things."

RJ nodded. "He's got to be watching from somewhere."

She fought an urge to glance over her shoulder. She wasn't sure she wanted RJ's dad watching the things she hoped to get up to with him tonight. Then again, maybe she should think more about how this would look to all the other people around them. What would RJ's siblings think of her spending the weekend with him? She worked closely with his brother Matthew in the office—would she be able to look him in the eye on Monday? And what about his mom? Would she see sleeping with his assistant as somehow beneath a Kincaid?

Of course Elizabeth Kincaid had much bigger problems to worry about right now. Partly due to information that she, Brooke Nichols, had provided to the police. She really needed to get that off her chest. Maybe now was a good time. She could casually say she'd seen his mom in the building and then… No.

Better to say the police had interviewed her and she just happened to mention—

"I'm glad you're here with me." RJ's soft voice jolted her from her fevered ruminations. He handed her a cool glass of clear white wine and she took a hasty sip. The moment for telling him had passed. Now he was getting romantic and she'd ruin it all if she said anything. "I've been wanting to come up here for a while, but didn't know how I'd feel."

"How do you feel?" She squeezed her guilt back down. He wanted a relaxing weekend, not more to worry about. It was probably better if she didn't mention it until they were back in the everyday world of Charleston.

"Okay. It's as beautiful as ever, peaceful and a perfect escape from reality."

"Can you ever really escape from reality?" Somehow it kept sneaking back into her consciousness.

"Sure." He smiled. "You file it away in a drawer."

"The third drawer down, perhaps?"

"Maybe that one, maybe another. Maybe more than one." He raised a brow. "Then you lock it and lose the key until some later date."

"That does not sound like the RJ I know."

He laughed. "It doesn't, does it? Maybe I'm trying to change."

"I don't think you should change." She said it in earnest, then wondered if she'd revealed too much about herself. "You're up-front and honest. You tackle things head-on and don't beat around the bush or try to people-please."

"And you've been the victim, more often than not."

"I'd much rather have you tell me what you think than have to guess it."

"I suppose that's one thing I got from my dad." His expression darkened. "Or I thought I did. He was blunt and truthful, and I never doubted a word he said." He swirled his glass of wine and peered into its depths. "Now I can see I should have been wary of all the things he left unsaid. Maybe you can never really know anyone."

"I don't suppose you can, but most people don't have secret families, so I don't think you could have seen it coming." It was hard to know what to say without overstepping the mark.

"No? My mom knew about them, and she kept quiet, too."

"She was probably trying to protect you from pain."

"Instead, she accidentally set herself up as a possible murderer." He shook his head and took a swig from his wine. "There's no justice in this world."

Brooke's stomach clenched. She hated to see RJ sounding so bitter. He was usually the most upbeat and positive person she knew. "There will be justice, but it might take some time."

"I wish I believed you. How can there be justice in a world where the Kincaid Group, the company I've devoted my working life to, is now forty-five percent owned by a half brother—" he said the word with a growl "—that I never knew existed." He looked up at her, eyes cold. "And who despises my entire family and the company he's just been handed."

Brooke put her wineglass down on the island. "It's all very strange and hard to understand right now." How could his father have been so cruel as to take away the company RJ saw as his birthright and hand it to an unknown rival?

"You know what?" RJ's voice was low with anger. "I do want to see what's in that third drawer. I want to see exactly what Dad wrote that would help me to understand why he stopped seeing me as his eldest son and heir." He slammed open the third drawer down on one side of the kitchen island. "Napkins and napkin rings. Can you see the significance?"

Brooke swallowed. She wanted to laugh, just to ease the tension, but it wasn't funny. "Did he have a desk?"

"Yes, there's a study." He strode from the room. Brooke glanced at the oven and saw the ribs still needed a few minutes. Always the trusty assistant, she followed him.

RJ marched into a bright study with cathedral ceilings and a leather-topped desk. "Ha. Two rows of three drawers." He pulled open one bottom drawer and rifled through the interior. "Bullet casings, ballpoint pens, paper clips, a broken golf tee." He slammed it and pulled open the other. "Reginald Kincaid letterhead and matching envelopes." He lifted the papers. "What's this?" He pulled out a manila envelope. "It has his name on the front. Or my name—since according to my birth certificate I'm Reginald Kincaid, as well." The envelope was sealed. Thick too, like it had a wad of papers, or even an object. "It's heavy."

"Are you going to open it?"

RJ hesitated, weighing it in his hand. The oven timer beeped in the kitchen.

Four

"I'll go check the ribs." Brooke seemed relieved at the excuse to leave him alone. Once she'd gone, RJ glanced down at the envelope in his hands. The writing was his father's familiar script, neat and commanding. He slid a finger under the sealed flap and ripped the paper carefully, aware he was frowning.

Then he lowered the open envelope to the desktop and eased the contents out onto the desk. Papers, mostly, a pair of cuff links, a ring he'd never seen his dad wear and some old photographs.

"They're done. I'll just toss the salad," called Brooke from the kitchen.

"Great." What was this envelope of things supposed to mean? He picked up the ring and looked at the design. Gold with a flat top, it was shaped almost like a class ring. As he stared at the shield he realized it was probably from his dad's time in special forces.

He recognized the bird holding a lightning bolt. The ring was worn, the gold scratched by use, but he didn't remember ever seeing it on his dad's finger. A relic from another lifetime, the lifetime in which Angela had been the woman he loved—and unbeknownst to him, the mother of his firstborn son.

"It's ready." Brooke's voice tugged him back to the present.

There was a lovely woman waiting for him in the other room, and painful memories could wait. He pushed the items back into the envelope and slid them into the same drawer. "Coming."

Brooke looked so beautiful standing silhouetted against the last rays of light. Her lush body beckoned to him, promising an evening filled with pleasure. Much better to tuck all that other stuff away in a drawer for now.

"Looks delicious." He stared directly at her as he said it.

A pretty smile played around her pink mouth. "It sure does. Where do you want to eat?"

"There's a table on the deck." He served the ribs onto two plates, and Brooke spooned out the salad and noodles. He grabbed cutlery from a drawer, picked up the wine and glasses with one hand, and Brooke brought the plates. The last rays of sun lit the polished wood table and chairs in a fiery reddish gold. He lit the decorative hurricane lamps with the BBQ lighter, and topped up their wine.

"Okay, this really is paradise." Brooke couldn't stop staring at the view. "This must be the only house for miles around."

"There are cabins and people out there, they're just hidden by the trees."

"The trees are kind to cloak everyone in peace and privacy." Her sweet smile made his chest fill with emotion.

"They're in charge around here. Dad always said that coming up to the mountains put everything into perspective. Problems shrink away and so does the human ego."

Brooke laughed. "I can't picture your father saying that."

"He could be quite introspective when the mood caught him." He could tell Brooke was rather intrigued by the new side of him she'd seen lately. Usually he didn't think too much about the impression he made on people, but right now it pleased him to show Brooke he wasn't just a hard-partying playboy. "It's easy to see why, now we know his life was a lot more complicated than any of us imagined." He took a bite of his food.

Being out here in the mountains brought a sense of equanimity that dulled the pain of recent events. He could think and talk about his dad calmly. Brooke's peaceful presence helped. He couldn't imagine her getting upset about anything. She was always the voice of reason in the office, ready to pour oil on troubled waters. "Did I ever thank you for taking me by the scruff of the neck and getting me out of trouble the other day?"

"When I marched you to your office and plied you with liquor?" Her pretty green eyes sparkled.

"Yes, that. A wise executive move."

"More an act of desperation. Still, I'd like to be an executive one day."

"You'd be good. You have an instinct for how to deal with people—getting them to deliver weekly updates so we know where everyone stands, for example."

"I got the idea from a management video I watched."

"I had no idea such bold ambition burned in your chest." RJ took a swig of wine. Brooke probably was wasted as his assistant, much as it pained him to admit it. HR had recently informed him that she'd submitted her application for a management role in the Events department and he'd told them he couldn't spare her right now. He needed an assistant he could trust with all that was going on in the wake of his father's death. Still, holding her back for his own reasons was selfish. He'd have to look around the company for the right role for her.

Brooke's sparkle had dimmed slightly. "I hope I didn't overstep the mark. I do really enjoy working with you."

"Of course you're looking to the future. I'm glad to hear you have big plans. You have a lot to offer the business world." He was relieved to see her lips curve into a smile again. "We'll have to talk about your future when things settle down."

She nodded. He felt a twinge of guilt that he didn't want to talk about her future right now, but frankly that was too big, complicated and potentially disturbing a subject for what was supposed to be a relaxing weekend in the mountains.

They chatted more innocuously about Charleston and their favorite music while the sun set and plunged them into the familiar velvety darkness. They swept the plates and glasses back inside. "Should we wash the dishes?" Brooke glanced at them where they lay on the counter. RJ had already disappeared into the next room.

"Don't worry about them. Come relax."

Brooke shrugged and followed him into the living room. It was hard to remember she was his guest, not his assistant right now. She hated leaving loose ends but maybe that was part of becoming the kind of person who managed others, rather than one who did everything themselves. RJ had changed the conversation rather deftly after her mention that she'd like to go into management, but maybe he just didn't want to be reminded of the office when he was trying to relax.

RJ leaned over a sleek device, and suddenly the room filled with music. Ella Fitzgerald, mellow and sultry. He looked up and smiled. "I thought we should dance."

Excitement stirred in her chest, along with a flutter of nerves. "Sure."

Dancing would get them close. Closeness would get them… RJ wound his arms around her waist. She could feel the heat of his body through his thin shirt. His back muscles moved under her hands as they swayed to the music. He pulled her against him and soon the rise and fall of her breath matched his. Or was it the other way around?

The song ended and another started, while they moved slowly around the big room. Dancing this way with RJ felt oddly natural, unhurried and relaxing. Arousal crept through her like wine, making her giddy but happy. They didn't even kiss until the third song started. RJ's lips brushed hers. Their mouths melded together slowly, tongues meeting and mingling.

Her chest pressed against his, her nipples tightening

against his hard muscle. Their hips swayed in rhythm and his hands roamed over her back. By the fifth song the kiss deepened to the point where their feet stopped moving. She felt RJ's fingers tugging at the hem of her shirt, then sliding over her skin. She shivered with pleasure and let her fingers roam into his waistband.

Soon they were plucking at each other's shirt buttons and pressing bare skin to bare skin. The music wrapped around them as RJ guided her onto the sofa and together they eased off her jeans. Her body throbbed with desire that gave urgency to her movements. The zipper of his pants got stuck as she tried to undo it and she found herself struggling with desperation that would be funny if she wasn't so…desperate!

RJ took over and together they shed his pants then wrapped themselves into each other on the wide surface of the sofa. RJ's big body fit perfectly around hers. His muscled arms held her close and his strong legs and hard abs made her pulse quicken.

Was she really lying semi-naked on a sofa with RJ Kincaid? Perhaps this was one of her more elaborate fantasies getting out of hand?

But his hot breath on her neck felt so real. So did the broad fingers slipping inside her delicate panties, and the lips closing over her nipples through the lace of her bra. Brooke gasped when he sucked on her nipple and sensation shot through her. She pushed her fingers into his thick hair and gave herself over to the sensation, arching her back and pressing her pelvis against him.

They both still wore their underwear, but she could feel RJ's intense arousal through his cotton boxers, and soon found her hands pushing down the elastic waistband and reaching for his erection. She shivered when she discovered how hard he was, how ready.

“Let’s go into the bedroom.” RJ’s voice was thick with need. Without waiting for her response he picked her up in his strong arms and carried her across the room. Supported by his strong body, Brooke felt weightless and desirable. RJ swept her into his bedroom, and laid her gently on the soft duvet.

“You’re so beautiful.” His gaze roamed over her body, making her skin tingle with excitement. He caressed her skin, starting at her shoulder and trailing his fingertips over her lacy bra and along her waist. When he reached her skimpy panties he hooked a finger into each side and slid them slowly over her legs, devouring her with his gaze as he pulled them down to her toes.

Excitement built in her chest as she waited for him to finish. Then he rose back over her and she leaned forward while he unhooked her bra and released her breasts. He kissed each freshly bared nipple and cooled it with a flash of his tongue. Breath coming faster, she pushed his boxers down over his thighs.

At last they were both naked. RJ climbed over her, kissing her face and murmuring how pretty her eyes were, and how soft her hair. The simple compliments made her feel like a goddess. She let her fingers roam over the thick, roping muscles of his arms and back and wished she could find words to admire them, but words deserted her as sensation overtook her body.

He entered her very gently, kissing her as he sank deep. Brooke arched against him, relishing the feel of him inside her, his powerful arms wrapped around her. The weight of his body settled over her, pushing her into the mattress as she clung to him.

"Oh, RJ." The words slipped from her mouth as she brushed his rough cheek with her lips. She'd waited years for this moment. She could feel him inside her, hard, yet so gentle as he moved with her.

A shiver of pleasure crept over her as he slid deeper, and she felt herself opening up to him. She snuck a peek at his face, and their eyes met in a single, electric moment. The expression on his face was almost pained, so intense, his blue eyes stormy with emotion.

Brooke felt her heart swell with feeling for this man. So strong and capable, he led the company with such energy and pride, and at this moment his entire being focused on her. His arms wrapped around her, enveloping her in their protective warmth, while he moved with precision and passion.

"You're an amazing woman, Brooke." His whispered words stirred something deep inside her. He shifted slightly, sending arrows of pleasure darting through her. Was she amazing? She certainly felt special right now.

Or were they both just caught up in the moment? Or in the madness that had brought her into his arms that night in his office.

A ripple of fear made her hold him tighter. "I'm not amazing." She couldn't bear for him to be making love to some imaginary woman who had nothing to do with the real Brooke Nichols. "I'm just…me."

RJ paused for a moment and their eyes met. Again that fierce gaze almost stole her breath. "You're amazing because you are just exactly you. The most beautiful, capable, sweet, organized, sexy and irresistible woman I've ever met."

A giggle rose in her chest. "That's quite a mix of adjectives."

"You're a unique person." He brushed soft kisses over her cheek and the bridge of her nose, making her smile. "And it's my very great pleasure to be sharing this bed with you." His penis stirred inside her, sparking a ripple of laughter along with a rush of erotic pleasure.

Her eyes slid closed as she kissed him on the mouth, drinking in the rich taste of him. She'd imagined moments like this, but not that she'd feel so totally swept away on a tide of intense pleasure.

RJ's strong arms eased them into a new position where she was sitting in his lap. As they moved together, the powerful penetration took her deeper into the mysterious otherworld they shared. RJ's hands on her skin, his thighs wrapped around her, his hair brushing her forehead…

Feelings raced through her. She wanted to shout, or cry. *I love him.* The thought flashed in her brain and she held him tighter. *Is it just my body talking?* Her brain grappled with powerful emotion while her body clung to his, moving with him in a thick sea of pleasure.

I love you, RJ.

She let her mind release the thought, though she didn't allow her lips to voice it. It was enough for her to know. She didn't want to throw pressure at him and ruin this beautiful moment. She'd never felt closer to anyone, and maybe she never would again.

For now, it was precious.

Her climax crept over her gradually, starting with

little waves that lapped at her fingers and toes, and ending in a big breaker that crashed over her.

RJ joined her, exploding with a gruff cry, crushing her against his chest and pressing his face to hers as they collapsed back on the bed. Overwhelmed by sensation and emotion, she lay limp in his arms.

"I don't remember the last time I felt this good." RJ cradled her, stroking her softly. "You're a miracle."

Brooke's chest, already bursting with happiness, almost exploded. Being here with RJ felt so absolutely right. It seemed odd that they hadn't come together earlier, when they were so perfect for each other. He stroked her cheek and she sighed. She'd made RJ feel good, too. Maybe that was the best part of all.

Lying here in his embrace she could imagine them living happily as a couple. They'd worked together successfully for five years, which was quite an accomplishment already. They'd always got on and never argued, and he obviously respected her opinion. "I'm glad I dragged you out of that meeting and plied you with liquor."

"Me, too. Not many people would have dared." He kissed her cheek softly and nuzzled against her. Again her chest swelled with joy. "You're a brave woman, Brooke Nichols."

She was, wasn't she? Not many women would chance a weekend away with their boss. For a moment the familiar doubts started to creep back in. How would they behave at the office? Would he be affectionate or would they go back to professional cordiality? What would she do if he kissed her in front of the other employees?

She blushed just thinking about it. She'd love it, of

course. She'd be so proud and happy to be RJ Kincaid's girlfriend. A dream come true. And here she was, living it.

They kissed, then dressed and went to enjoy more music and dancing, then undressed and made love again. This time they fell asleep together, with seductive music still throbbing away in the living room. Brooke slept deeply, totally relaxed and at ease in RJ's arms.

In the morning she awoke with an odd mix of anticipation and anxiety. They had two whole days to spend together with no interruptions.

Then again, what if they had nothing to talk about? What if he grew bored with her?

"Morning, gorgeous." RJ pressed a kiss to the back of her neck.

"Hi." A wave of pleasure lapped over her at the touch of his lips and her doubts scattered. "Did you sleep okay?"

"Never slept better in my life. You're the best medicine in the world."

She smiled. "I'm glad. Last night was fun."

He kissed her cheek. "More than fun. You're full of surprises, Brooke."

"I am?"

"I had no idea you had such a sensual side."

"I try to keep it under wraps when I'm at the office." She winked. "Might not be appropriate."

"There's a whole different Brooke that I never knew about."

"Actually I think the Brooke you know is about ninety percent of the real Brooke." She didn't want him to start thinking she was really a temptress superspy or something, and then be disappointed. "There are just a few facets of me best not viewed under fluorescent lighting."

RJ glanced down at her body and lifted the covers to reveal a peaked pink nipple. "I think you'd look amazing under any lighting."

The way he stared at her made her feel beautiful. She worked hard to keep her body in reasonably good shape, but she'd never felt ultra gorgeous—until RJ's appreciative blue gaze touched her skin.

She trailed a finger over his muscled chest. "I'm not sure what I expected under all that crisp suiting, but let's just say I can tell you work out."

"I play a lot of tennis and squash. They're a full-body workout."

"I used to play tennis in high school." She said it shyly. She'd been their team's star player, but never pursued it in college since she didn't want to take too much time away from her studies and she needed to work almost full-time.

"No kidding? We'll have to hit some balls together. We can go to the club when we get back."

The club? The ultra-exclusive country club that cost over fifty thousand dollars a year just for the privilege of membership? She swallowed. "I haven't played in years. I probably wouldn't even be able to hit the ball over the net."

"We'll have to find out, won't we? Tennis is like riding a bicycle, at least I think so. After ten minutes or so you'll feel like you never put down your racquet."

"Maybe, if you promise to take it easy on me." She slid her finger down over his hard belly, which contracted under her touch.

"I don't know. That's not really the Kincaid way."

"You're more into crushing your opponents then dancing over their shattered remains?" That was their business reputation to a certain extent. RJ looked surprised. Had she stepped over an unspoken boundary by talking about the family? "I don't mean that literally, of course. Just that I—"

RJ laughed. "Don't back down now. That's exactly what I meant. We're not able to lose gracefully. It's not in our DNA. If we were, maybe we'd be able to fit in better with crusty old Charleston society, where you need to suck up to someone whose great-great-granny came over on the *Mayflower* just so you'll get invited to their garden parties. We're constitutionally unable to do that."

"But the Kincaids are part of Charleston society."

He laughed again. "As if there was only one Charleston society. Believe me, there are plenty of people in this town who look down on the Kincaids as nouveau riche upstarts who won't be around for long." He looked thoughtful. "It's never bothered me before, but with everything that's going on lately I'm more determined than ever to prove them wrong."

"The Kincaid Group will weather this storm. So far it doesn't seem so much worse than the time we lost the Martin account."

"The Martins went out of business. This time people are leaving just because they can, and they're going to the competition."

"So, you'll have to show them what they're missing. And now's a good time to build up the company's real-estate portfolio."

"It is. We've been moving assets in that direction.

When the real estate market comes back we'll be sitting on a gold mine, especially along the Charleston waterfront. Hey, why are we lying here naked talking business?"

"Because we're that kind of people." She smiled at him.

He lifted a dark brow. "We're a lot alike."

Brooke shrugged. She wasn't sure how alike they really were. Not being accepted into the highest echelons of Charleston society had never been one of her most pressing problems. And a relationship with her would hardly boost his social standing, which apparently was a big concern for him.

"We are alike." He obviously sensed her doubts. "We're both teetering on the brink of being workaholics, we like good restaurants, we play a mean game of tennis and we're both lying in this bed."

Brooke chuckled. "When you put it like that... But you're making a lot of assumptions about my game of tennis."

"I know you well enough to know you wouldn't have mentioned it unless you were practically on the tour."

"I'll have to be careful what I tell you. You have dangerously high expectations."

"Only because you never disappoint." He said it plainly, no hint of teasing.

"Never? Surely I've made a few typos along the way."

"I sincerely doubt it, but I'm talking about you as a person, not an office appliance. Don't think I haven't noticed how brilliant you are."

Brooke beamed inside. "I enjoy a challenge."

"And I enjoy you." He nibbled her earlobe gently,

sending a rush of sensation through her. Suddenly they were kissing again, then twisted up in the duvet making mad, early morning love.

Love? No. Not that. Having crazy, wild, before-breakfast sex. She'd never had so much sex in a twenty-four-hour period, and they were barely twelve hours in. Energetic and passionate, RJ soon brought her to new heights of arousal and excitement. They climaxed together, with a lot of noise, followed by laughter as they tried to disentangle themselves from the duvet.

"I'd suggest we shower together," said RJ, once they stopped panting long enough to form a sentence. "But I'm worried we may never make it to breakfast."

"What are we doing for breakfast? I don't recall too much breakfast food in the fridge."

"That's because there's an excellent diner up the road, and I always go there. You'll love it. It's a real slice of life in the mountains. I'll shower first, then leave you with some privacy."

Brooke couldn't resist sneaking a few long, lascivious peeks as RJ rose from the bed and strode naked across the room. His body was magnificent. Broad shoulders tapered to a slim waist, and his backside... ooh la la. She would probably never be able to keep a straight face in the office again.

She fanned herself as she heard the rush of water in the shower. She'd expected RJ to be a romantic charmer, but not that he'd drive her so completely over the edge. Maybe all the years of fantasizing about him in secret made their actual coming together so intense.

She loved that he was so affectionate. He seemed to really enjoy holding and hugging her, as well as kissing and licking and all that other good stuff. And, boy, was he deft at sliding a condom on at just the right moment. He didn't even need to interrupt the flow of events. He must have had the packet ripped open before they even started.

She frowned. This should remind her that he was no innocent boy next door on his first date. RJ Kincaid had bedded a lot of women, and she wasn't likely to be the last.

Her chest tightened, then she realized how foolish it was to be thinking about the future when they still had the whole weekend ahead of them. She had no idea what the future would bring. Who could have predicted that Reginald Kincaid, one of the most vibrant men she'd ever met, would be shot dead by a mystery assailant, let alone that his wife would be accused of his murder?

Brooke let out a long sigh. If only she could figure out who else might be responsible. She was in the office on the night of the murder and left less than half an hour before it happened. The police had even interviewed her as if she was a suspect at first. Whoever killed him might have been in the building the entire time. But who?

"Why the serious face?" RJ appeared in the doorway, toweling off his spectacular bronzed body.

Already she felt a smile creep across her lips. Who could stay serious when confronted with such a vision? "What serious face?"

"Much better."

They ate an enormous breakfast in the 1950s-style diner, served by the owner who had probably been doling out grits since the 1950s. He made a big fuss of both RJ and Brooke, treating them like visiting royalty. His great-granddaughter, aged about seven, brought them flowers she'd picked in the garden and handed the bouquet to Brooke. "You're very pretty."

Brooke smiled. "You're very pretty, too. And I'm impressed with the standard of service here. You don't get flowers and compliments every day with breakfast." When the little girl had skipped back outside she whispered, "I wonder if they pay her to flatter the guests."

"It's a good strategy. Maybe The Kincaid Group should try it out on our customers." Humor twinkled in his eyes. "On the other hand, most of our clients aren't nearly as easy on the eyes so it might come across as phony."

"Oh, please." She wanted to protest that she wasn't pretty, but she didn't want to appear to be fishing for more compliments. She'd certainly never felt prettier in her life. "I hope you don't have anything too strenuous planned for this morning. I'm not sure I'll be able to move after that fantastic meal." Perfectly crisp bacon, golden scrambled eggs, freshly baked rolls and spicy fried potato. And the ubiquitous bowl of grits.

"We'll save the hike to the summit for this afternoon then. How about we stroll to the lake and pretend we're fishing?"

"Sounds good."

She had no idea how good. While they'd been relaxing in the diner, a member of staff had packed the trunk of the Suburban with an icebox of chilled beer and a packed lunch.

"I feel like elves are following close behind us waiting on us hand and foot."

"Just takes a little organizing."

Again, Brooke wondered if he did this sort of thing often. Bringing girls up to the cabin and scheming with all the locals to pamper and spoil them. Maybe right now the people in the diner were shaking their heads and clucking their tongues and discussing how long "this one" would last.

How long would it last?

RJ opened her car door, always the perfect gentleman. Right now she didn't feel like his admin at all. It was almost impossible to imagine showing up at the office on Monday and going through his in-box. On the other hand she could imagine any number of intriguing things that could happen between now and Monday.

RJ seemed like a different person than when they left. For the first time since his father's death he appeared truly relaxed, his face crinkling into smile lines rather than the frown he'd worn so much lately. His broad shoulders looked at ease, not tight with tension.

She felt different, too. Their night of passion had awakened something inside her. She was no virgin but she'd certainly never experienced pleasure like that before. This morning she'd grown into a more deeply sensual person than she was yesterday. Colors were brighter and smells sweeter and even the air tasted bright and crisp as champagne.

By Monday they'd both be different people, one way or another. Her fantasy of a relationship with RJ was coming true and happiness seemed right within her grasp.

Though if it didn't work out, if this weekend was all they had, she'd have the agony of knowing just what she was missing—for the rest of her life.

Five

A lazy morning of casting flies from a grassy riverbank, followed by their luxurious picnic, led to a relaxed walk in the woods. RJ was easy to talk to. Which was hardly a surprise given that she'd known him for years. It was odd, and wonderful, how quickly and totally their relationship had altered from being purely professional to...utterly unprofessional.

They carried a thick foam camping pad out onto the broad balcony of the cottage, and now lay on it, naked, covered only by a thin sheet swiped from the linen closet. Warm spring air caressed their skin, still damp from the exertions of a heated afternoon lovemaking session. RJ traced patterns on her belly with a lazy finger, stirring little rivers of sensation that made her want to giggle.

His hair, tousled at some point by her fingers, hung

down to his eyes, which shone, dark with arousal. "Maybe we shouldn't ever go back."

Brooke's stomach contracted slightly under his fingers. "Tempting as that sounds…"

"Come on. Would they really miss us?" Humor deepened his dimples. "That unpleasant Jack Sinclair can take over running the company and you and I can just live in the woods on trout."

"We didn't catch any trout." The idea held marvelous appeal. No more early morning commutes. No more taking minutes in meetings. But at heart she was a practical girl. "We didn't even see any trout."

RJ's grin was infectious. "Berries, then."

"Okay, berries. Supplemented with orders from your favorite restaurant." She played with the lock of dark hair on his forehead.

RJ planted a kiss on her stomach. "I've never contemplated any other life than the one I was born to. Lately, though, with all this madness surrounding the family and the company, I can't help thinking that there are other possibilities out there." His expression darkened somewhat. "And that in making his will my dad was giving me permission to explore them."

Was he serious? She couldn't imagine The Kincaid Group without RJ, or RJ without the company that seemed to be his lifeblood.

But she wanted to be supportive. "What would you like to do, if you could do anything?"

RJ traced the line of her thigh with his broad thumb. "I think I'm doing it." His mischievous expression teased her. "And maybe I could branch out into this." He lowered his head and licked her nipple, tightening it to a hard peak. "And this." He raised his mouth to hers and kissed her with exquisite tenderness.

Brooke's heart swelled inside a chest already very full with the wonder and excitement of their new relationship. RJ spoke as if he'd just discovered the love of his life—her.

Don't get carried away! Up here in the clouds it was easy to forget all about the real world, but sooner or later they'd have to go back to it.

After another delicious dinner from the bounty in the fridge they watched a classic Hitchcock movie together. RJ held her tight during the scary bits and Brooke loved enjoying such a normal, everyday couple activity with the man who'd once seemed wholly unobtainable. After the movie they shared a dish of caramel ice cream, then kissed with cold tongues and warm hearts.

Sunday was a lazy day. They didn't even rise from bed until nearly noon, and only then because RJ decided it was time to confront the manila envelope of memories his father had left him.

RJ brought a new sense of calm back into the study with him. He'd closed the door on Friday night determined to enjoy his weekend with Brooke. By Sunday, however, a sliver of guilt was intruding on their shared paradise. Sunday dinner was a Kincaid tradition. They all gathered in the big family home and shared a traditional roast or some other delicacy their mom had conjured up. Now she was in jail, the family tradition was temporarily suspended. How could they face each other across the table with neither the matriarch nor the patriarch of the family present?

Their dad would never sit there again. They'd stubbornly kept the tradition going at their mom's insistence in the weeks and months since his death. It was no doubt his responsibility as the eldest to gather the clan in their mom's absence, but he didn't have the heart.

He'd spent two enjoyable days here on the outskirts of his life, with the lovely Brooke for company. But he had decisions to make and avoiding them didn't sit well with him.

Brooke had cooked pancakes from a packet mix while he made coffee, and after they'd eaten she tactfully excused herself, saying she needed time to make a couple of phone calls. She went out on the terrace, where the reception was strongest, and he headed back into his father's inner sanctum with a heavy heart.

The envelope lay there in the drawer where he'd left it. He wondered if his dad had prepared it all at once in a typical flourish of brusque efficiency, or if its contents were the product of hours of thought, packing and unpacking.

Probably the former. With a swift inhale he pulled the packet from the drawer and emptied its contents on the desk in a rude clatter and rustle. Amongst the yellowed papers was a crisp, new sheet, folded in two. RJ snatched it off the desk and pulled it open. His scalp pricked with discomfort as he saw the handwritten lines. Another letter. The letter he'd opened and read so hastily after the funeral had cut a dark scar in his heart and he suspected this would only reopen and deepen the wound.

While you bear my name, you are in truth not my firstborn son.

He'd seen Angela and her sons at his father's funeral, but refused to believe the gossip about who they were. When he opened the letter, that one brief line had knocked away the foundation of his life. So swift and brutal was the blow that he'd been hard-pressed to act like himself for the rest of the day. He no longer was himself. Since birth he'd been Reginald Kincaid, Jr., chip off the old block. All he'd wanted was to be just like his dad, a proud family man, successful in business and in everything else he turned his hand to, from fighting foreign wars to scoring birdies on the club golf course.

In that letter his father had revealed he was not the man they'd all assumed him to be. Fathering a child before his marriage was one thing—and as he'd posthumously explained, he didn't know about his son Jack until years after his birth—but resuming his relationship with his son's mother and maintaining them as a second family went beyond the common accusation of adultery and into the realm of almost criminal deception.

Steeling himself, he focused on the handwritten script that covered most of two pages.

Dear Reginald,

We all make choices in life and, as you are by now well aware, I made choices that many would disapprove of. You may well be angry with me, and knowing your proud and honest spirit, I bet you are. You've had some time to think about how all this affects you, and above all I want to make you aware that you have choices, too.

RJ growled. Did his father think he was some beardless sixteen-year-old looking for a pep talk? He'd been a man himself now for a decade and a half.

My parents took away my choices when they forbid me to marry Angela, the woman I loved.

RJ suppressed a curse. How he wished he'd never heard the name of Angela Sinclair, or her accursed son.

Being an obedient son, I didn't marry her. Instead I ran away from them all, from all of their plans and hopes and dreams for me. As you know, my time in the service was a defining period in my life that shaped me like a blade in the furnace, and I look back on it with pride as well as regret. I'm enclosing the ring I wore for many years as a symbol of my commitment to my unit. It was a wedding ring of sorts, when I wore it, as I had thrown away all other allegiances. I sought to escape my former life and forge a new one all my own. I also enclose the pilot's license I earned all those years ago and that you used to tease me about. As you can see, it really does exist, along with the other, less savory, realities of my life.

Escape is an illusion. No matter how far you run, or how fast, the truths of your life—of who you are and what you've done—dog your heels over all terrain, and sooner or later you have to turn and face them. When I returned home I had to face the parents who'd waited and worried every day I was gone. This time, obeying their wishes that I take a suitable bride and start a family seemed a far more livable kind of escape, and I soon met and married your wonderful mother. My happiness was complete and

I barely thought of the lives I'd left behind, until I learned by chance that the woman I once loved had borne my child and raised him in my absence.

By this time I had children of my own with your mother and knew the force, and felt the commitment, of the paternal bond. I hope you'll one day understand that there was no way I could turn my back on my own flesh and blood. When I met Angela again, I felt the full power of our grand passion that I'd tried so hard to leave behind in my attempts to be a good son.

Don't be a good son, RJ.

RJ blinked and thrust the letter down, growling with a mix of fury and disbelief. All his life he'd been proud to fulfill his parents' goals and dreams, to now be told it was all some kind of colossal mistake? He snatched the pages up again, anxious to get to the end.

All your life you've been told where to go and what to do. Your mother and I carefully chose the best schools and groomed you for your future role in The Kincaid Group. We never asked you what you wanted. RJ, my son, I want you to take this opportunity to look inside yourself and decide what you truly want from your life.

RJ threw the letter down with another curse. How arrogant of his father to assume that he'd blindly followed along with their plans for him. He'd been successful in school and in business and everything in between because of his own hard work and dedication and because he'd wanted to. He knew plenty of men with all his advantages who'd thrown them away and run off to pursue alternate dreams. His old pal Jake ran a beach bar in Jamaica, for Chrissakes. He could have dropped out of the Caine Academy, or flunked out of Duke and opened a surf shop. He hadn't done those things because he'd chosen the life he was living. He'd fully intended to spend his entire career building The Kincaid Group until his father decided to pull the rug out from under him.

He was nearly at the end of the letter anyway. Blood boiling with a mix of anger and frustration, he focused his eyes on the neat handwriting again.

> The defining fact of my life, son, is that I loved two women.

RJ shook his head. Surely love was an act of choice. In his opinion his dad should have told his parents to shove it and married Angela. Of course he would never have been born, but right now that didn't seem like such a bad deal.

> I never claimed Angela and our son during my life as my role in society was important to me. I wanted those invitations to the black tie affairs, the yacht club memberships and the satisfaction of being a leading member of Charleston society.

RJ snorted. *Thanks for setting fire to all that and leaving us in the ashes.*

His father had always put a lot of stock in what other people thought. More than a man of his standing should have to. It likely went back to the Kincaids never being on quite the upper tier of Charleston society. His mom's family was one of the old guard. In retrospect he could see that was probably the chief reason his dad married her. And now look where marriage to Reginald Kincaid had put her.

> I'm not proud of the choices I made. I've long carried the burden of keeping Angela and her sons secret. In making my will I tried to redress some of the wrongs I committed against Jack. He grew up on the sidelines of society, as the child of a single mother, and without many of the advantages you enjoyed. In giving him a majority share in The Kincaid Group I aimed to give him the opportunities he was denied as a boy. I realize this may seem unfair to you, but I also know you're wise enough to understand my reasoning and strong enough to forge ahead and make a success of your life, either in the company or outside it. If you're reading this letter it's because I'm dead, of natural causes or otherwise. I wrote it to explain myself to you after you'd had some time to reflect on the terms of the will, since knowing you as I do I suspect you tore up my first letter and threw it on the fire.
>
> I love you, RJ, and I'm proud of you.
>
> Dad.

RJ sank into the chair. His anger had evaporated, replaced by a wounding sorrow. Apparently his dad hadn't known him as well as he'd thought. Far from tearing up his first letter, he'd carried it with him since the day he received it. Maybe his dad really hadn't known how much he'd loved him? They'd never been much for words or hugs.

Angry as he was at the choices—no, the stupid mistakes—his father had made, he'd give almost anything to see him just one more time.

But life—and death—didn't work like that.

He folded the letter and thrust the ring, the license, the photos and other stray bits of paper that commemorated milestones in his dad's life, back into the envelope.

His dad had given him permission, perhaps encouragement, to leave The Kincaid Group if he wanted to. He could move away, start a new life in a different city.

A cold shiver ran through him at the limitless possibilities, the many routes his life could take. Right now the only thing he wanted was to see Brooke's lovely smile again.

"Brooke! You promised you'd tell me everything!" Evie's voice rose with exasperation.

Brooke moved the phone further from her ear. "I'm trying. The weekend's not even over yet. I'm sitting on a balcony with a ridiculous view over what must be the entire range of the Great Smoky Mountains." The morning "smoke" or fog had evaporated, leaving a crystal-clear vista of wooded slopes and sapphire blue sky. How could she even describe what she'd experienced over the last two days? "It's just a romantic weekend. You know what that's like." She wanted to downplay the whole thing. It was their first weekend together. Yes, it was fantastic. More than fantastic. But it didn't mean RJ would be shopping for a ring later.

"You had sex with him?"

"No, we meditated together."

"Oh, stop! Okay, that was a bit crude. You slept together."

"We did that, too. He's a very heavy sleeper, who makes this adorable purring noise right before he's about to wake up." A vision of his powerful chest rising and falling filled her brain. She'd watched him for over an hour, afraid that if she moved she'd wake him and spoil the pleasure of watching him sleep in her arms. He'd looked both powerful and vulnerable at the same time. Irresistible.

"Aw, like a big kitty. So when are you seeing him again?"

"I imagine I'll see him first thing tomorrow when I give him his mail." She swallowed. Would she be able to maintain her usual professional demeanor now that she knew exactly what he looked like beneath those elegant pin-striped suits? Now that he knew exactly what she looked like beneath her tailored skirts and blouses.

Her nipples pricked to attention as she remembered his blue gaze raking over her skin, drinking her in like a long, tall glass of water in the desert.

"Hmm, mad passionate love on the office desk, papers sliding forgotten to the floor while the phone rings."

"Definitely not." Brooke blushed at the vivid image her friend had conjured.

"Never say never. Would you have thought a week ago that you'd be locking lips in his office?"

"Not in a million years. I won't say I didn't fantasize about it, but I never thought it would happen."

"See? Anything could happen. Before the year is out you could be Mrs. Brooke Kincaid."

"I very much doubt it. The Kincaids are apparently obsessed with their social standing in Charleston. In addition to being illegitimate, I don't have a drop of blue blood in my veins. RJ's father didn't marry his mistress because she wasn't from the right social class, and from the sound of it not much has changed since then."

"Don't be silly. RJ's crazy about you, and he's far too self-assured to worry about other people's opinions of his lovely bride."

"Stop! I thought you were the one warning me to go slow in case it all ends in tears."

"The way I see it, you're in over your head already. Might as well enjoy it and worry about the tears later. Did you ever figure out what to get your mom for her birthday?"

Brooke gasped. "I can't believe it. I totally forgot! And it's tomorrow. No, it's today, Sunday! I haven't even called her. I'm supposed to be at her place for dinner."

Becoming involved with RJ had totally derailed her brain. She hung up and called her mom to confirm they were still on. As she was speaking, she heard the sliding door to the balcony whisper open, and RJ stepped out. She waved hi and finished the conversation, telling her mom to book a table wherever she wanted.

"I missed you." RJ's deep voice wrapped around her at the same time his arms did.

"We weren't apart more than twenty minutes."

"Felt like an eternity." He nuzzled her neck, then rested his head on her shoulder for a moment.

"Are you okay? Did you read the letter?"

She felt his chest rise as he sucked in a breath. "I read the letter. My dad apparently gives me permission to abandon all my responsibilities and seize a new life by the…" He looked up and his gaze met hers with blistering force. "All I can say is thank heaven for you being here in my arms right now."

"Don't let it get to you. Maybe we should go for a walk in the woods to blow off steam."

A sparkle of mischief crept into his eyes. "I can think of another way to blow off steam."

Brooke wasn't at all nervous on the flight back. Hand in hand with RJ, she felt they could stride across the world together and nothing could harm them.

Back in her condo, she shrugged out of the chic "country attire" she'd bought for her weekend in the woods, showered and dressed in something her mom would approve of. "You have such a nice body. You should let people see it." By people, she meant men. Barbara Nichols's life revolved around men and the chance of being admired by them.

She stopped by a mall and picked up the most expensive tennis bracelet she could find. Expensive was always good as her mom would know exactly how much it cost. When she arrived at 14 Pine Grove, as usual her mom was dressed for a night on the town. "Oh sweetheart, you shouldn't have!" The sparkly bracelet hit its mark, and was immediately added to the collection of bling on her thin wrist.

"Where's Timmy?" Her mom's boyfriend had been a regular fixture around the house for nearly two years.

"Moved to Charlotte."

"Why?"

"His job transferred him to their plant there." She shrugged as if she couldn't care less. Brooke could see the lines in her face had deepened.

"Oh, Mom, I know you two got along well. Did you talk at all about going to join him?"

Her mom's pale blue eyes had a hollow look. "He said he thought it was better if we made a clean break. He started talking about kids and you know how that goes." She swatted the air dismissively with her manicured hand. Timmy was at least fifteen years younger than her. This had happened before.

"I'm sorry to hear that, because I thought he was nice." Not interesting, or funny, or charming or gorgeous, like RJ, but he treated her mom well.

"Yeah, well. Sooner or later it's time to move on. Maybe we'll meet Mr. Right tonight. I booked us a table at Dashers, it's a new place just up the road."

Brooke's heart sank. The prospect of sitting at a bar booth, eyeing potentially eligible males with her mother, was enough to suck every last breath of wind from her sails. Again, this had happened before. Still, it was her birthday.

Twenty minutes later they sat in the shiny black booth, which looked just as Brooke had imagined it. Her mom's sculpted legs were artfully draped outside the booth where they could catch the eye of any passing males. "How about you, sweetheart? Are you still spending the weekends holed up in your apartment practicing yoga or do you ever go out into the world?"

All of Brooke's better judgment told her to keep quiet about RJ. "Actually I'm seeing someone." Apparently her better judgment had disappeared with her first sip of Frascati.

Her mom's mouth and eyes widened. "Who? Someone from work?"

Brooke gulped. "Um, yes, actually."

"Did you finally catch that gorgeous boss of yours?" She leaned in conspiratorially. "I'm always telling you you're beautiful enough for even the richest man in Charleston, if you'd just shine a light on your assets." She glanced approvingly at the cleavage revealed by her blouse. "You do have a glow about you, now I'm looking closer." Her penciled brow lifted. "Well, don't sit there in silence. Tell me more!"

Brooke took another sip of her wine. "It is my boss." She said it quietly. "RJ. He's been through a lot lately and I think I've been a shoulder to cry on for him."

"Oh God, not a crier! I can't stand them and they usually drink like fish, too."

Brooke laughed. Her mom had a way of disarming anyone's inhibitions. "Not literally. He's just been going through a lot. I'm sure you've seen the stories in the papers."

"About his mom killing his dad." She grimaced. "Nasty stuff."

"Mrs. Kincaid didn't do it, I'm sure of that."

"Papers said they have evidence that she was at the scene of the crime around the time that it happened. That sounds pretty guilty to me."

Brooke's back stiffened. Was her admission to the police that she'd seen Elizabeth Kincaid in the building shortly before the murder the entire reason RJ's mother had been arrested? She'd yet to hear of anything more concrete.

"She came to bring him his dinner or something. Probably, I mean. I don't know for sure." She didn't want anyone to know she was involved in the investigation. At least not until she'd found a chance to tell RJ. If only she could take back her words and tell the police she hadn't seen or heard anything. "She's a really nice lady. Very quiet and sweet."

Her mom clucked her tongue. "Those quiet ones. There's always more to them than meets the eye. You don't work in my business for more than thirty years without learning a thing or two about people." As a waitress, she claimed to have gained astonishing insight into the human psyche. "She probably smiled her way through decades of marriage, being the good little wife, then when the revelations about his second family came out, she snapped." She clapped her hands together and Brooke jumped in her seat.

"I'm sure it must have been someone else. But the problem is no one else has a real motive."

"What about that newly discovered son who inherited a whole lot of money?"

Brooke nodded. "He seems to have gained the most by Reginald's death. And I hear he's not very nice, either." She drew in a breath. "Don't tell anyone I said that, okay?" Her mom loved to gossip with the customers. "He is part of the family, after all. Or at least sort of."

"Bitter." Her mom puckered up her lips and took a sip of her Manhattan without leaving any lipstick on the glass. A skill she was proud of. "I bet you anything it was him that did it. But we seem to have gotten off track here." Her lips widened back into a smile. "Are you getting serious with Reginald Kincaid, Jr.?"

Brooke laughed. "It's RJ. No one calls him Reginald."

"Well, don't you let him get away. You won't get many opportunities like that in a lifetime."

"I don't know where it will lead, but I really like him."

"Don't let him treat you badly because he's a rich boy. Not that you would. My Brooke has a good head on her shoulders." Their plate of nachos arrived and her mom took one and crunched it. "I never got my big break. Not yet, anyway." She winked. "But it sounds like you'll soon be living in fine style."

"Mom!" Suddenly Brooke could picture her bragging to her customers about how her little Brooke was dating one of those big-shot Kincaids that were all over the papers. "Will you do me a huge favor and keep it to yourself, at least for a while?"

"And spoil all the fun of bragging about you? Aww." She pouted. "I'll do my best. You'd better get engaged quick, though, as I'm not sure I'll be able to hold my tongue for long."

"I have no idea if we'll ever get engaged. We only started dating this week."

"You could always try telling him you're pregnant." Her mom lifted a brow.

Brooke stiffened. "If that had worked for you we'd still be living with my father. As it is, I've never even met him."

Her mom drew in a breath. "You're right. I forgot. Now why did I ever tell you about that?"

"Because I kept asking until you broke down." Brooke smiled. "And you knew it was better for me to finally hear the truth rather than all those crazy stories about a traveling salesman who'd be back from the Far East any day now."

"Well, it sounded more exciting than a balding ex-quarterback who owns a shoe store in Fayetteville. I looked him up on Facebook and let me tell you he's not aging well. He sure was handsome in his day, though."

"And maybe he did us both a favor by letting you go." Her mom had tearfully admitted that he'd left town—for good—the day after she'd happily told him about her surprise pregnancy.

"We'd been dating for six months. I thought it was a sure thing." She shrugged her slim shoulders inside her silky dress. "But you never know what people are made of until their feet are to the fire."

"Well, RJ's feet are in several different fires right now, and I'm doing my best to be the water that cools them."

"Just make sure you don't get left to run down the drain when the fire's been put out. And you don't want to lose your job over him, either. One thing I've always prided myself on is keeping my job. Men come and go, but work will put food on the table if they're there or not, and don't you forget it."

"Don't worry." Brooke picked up a nacho and nibbled it thoughtfully. "I won't."

Six

"You took Brooke to the cabin?" RJ's brother Matt stared at him. They were alone in RJ's office with the door closed. "Things aren't so desperate that you need to work on weekends. I did score the new Larrimore Industries account after all, and that should start bringing in revenue as early as—"

"Matt! I didn't bring her there to type my memos."

He watched while understanding dawned in his brother's green eyes. "You and Brooke... Oh, RJ, are you sure that was a good idea? She's such a key member of the company and you know how you are with women."

RJ bristled. "Exactly how am I with women?"

"Enthusiastic."

"So now I'm enthusiastic about Brooke. She's beautiful, intelligent, kind and she gives great hugs." He couldn't stop a smile creeping across his mouth. Even thinking about Brooke gave him a warm glow. "There's quite a different side to her than the one we see at the office."

"I bet she's saying the same thing about you." Matt raised an eyebrow. "Are you going to be kissing in meetings and sneaking off for afternoon trysts?"

RJ fought a grin. "Appealing as that sounds, I think we'll both have enough self-control to maintain a semblance of professional decorum."

"And what happens when you get tired of her?"

"Unimaginable."

"Maybe I have a more vivid imagination than you. I know what it's like when a relationship starts to sour. You do realize she could sue you for sexual harassment and win?"

RJ frowned. "Brooke would never do that."

"Let's hope not. We can't afford another scandal right now. I guess you'll just have to marry her." There was not the slightest glimmer of humor in his brother's steady gaze.

RJ's stomach tightened. "Let's not get too carried away. We haven't even been dating for a full week, yet."

"See? That's the RJ I know. You're crazy about them for a while, then something better comes along."

"These days I never know what's going to happen next, so I'm going to seize the moment. Did you guys visit Mom over the weekend?"

"Both days, just like we promised. She says she's doing fine but she's looking rather thin and drawn. We've got to get her out of there."

"I've been on the phone to the D.A.'s office every day. Three times today already. If they have evidence they need to produce it. You can't keep someone behind bars without a trial in this country. It's not like she's accused of an act of terrorism." He felt his hackles rising again. "The assistant D.A. said something about a witness at the scene, but then she clammed up. I know there wasn't an eyewitness to the murder or we'd have heard about it. If there was, we'd know what the hell happened and Mom would be home where she belongs. The private detective I hired is trying to break down the blue wall of silence that is our local police department right now, but no luck so far."

"Lily's going to visit her again this afternoon."

"I'm going, too, after the meeting. I bought some of her favorite chocolates." He shook his head. "Though I'm sure even Ghirardelli doesn't taste all that great when you're locked up in a tiny cell sleeping next to a toilet. It makes me sick."

"I know, RJ. Honestly, I understand about the Brooke thing. This nightmare is hard on all of us and I can see the temptation to fall into the nearest pair of soft arms." He clapped RJ on the shoulder. "Let me know if you hear anything new from the police or the D.A.'s office, okay?"

"Will do."

Brooke darted away from RJ's office door and back to her desk, heart pounding, before Matthew emerged.

He looked right at her and smiled, and she managed to stammer a greeting, sure her face was red as fire. She'd been unable to resist listening in on RJ's conversation with Matt—horribly unprofessional, not to mention totally uncool, but she couldn't help herself. She'd pretended to rearrange some files in the tall cabinet next to his door, but every nerve in her brain and body was fine-tuned to pick up all sound from inside.

Her heart had soared as RJ said such sweet things about her, then crashed when Matt muttered about lawsuits and accused him of falling into the nearest pair of soft arms. That rang painfully true. None of them knew where this was going, and it could be heading to a lot of very dark places.

The door was now wide open, and she glanced inside to see RJ, head bent over some papers on his desk. He looked up. “Are you going to sue me for sexual harassment?”

“Never.” She said it too fast and too loud. Did he know she’d been listening?

“Never say never.” RJ raised a brow. “You could, you know.”

She walked into his office and closed the door gently behind her. “What happened between us was entirely mutual.” She kept her voice composed and professional, though her heart was hammering. How typical of RJ to come right out and say what anyone else would want to brush under the carpet. Right now she adored him more than ever. “I don’t regret it.”

Though maybe I will one day.

RJ rose and came around the desk. In his dark suit he looked imposing and elegant. Different from the rugged charm of the RJ she’d enjoyed all weekend, but every bit as irresistible. He wrapped his arms gently around her waist and pulled her close for a kiss. Her insides bubbled with pleasure and she let her hands slide under his suit jacket and caress his back through his cotton shirt.

“This is fun.” RJ’s breath heated her neck.

"It feels naughty."

"It is naughty." He squeezed her backside gently. "And I could think of even naughtier things we could do."

She giggled. "Don't you have a ten o'clock?"

"I'm the executive vice president. I can cancel it." His deadly serious expression only made her want to laugh harder.

"It's with a potential new client." She ran a finger along his shirt buttons. "A large manufacturing company with factories in China."

"Hmm. You're making this all very confusing and difficult for me."

"Then as your personal assistant I'll have to insist that you go to the meeting."

"Can you do that?"

"Apparently I just did." She kissed his dimple. "Though only time will tell if you listen." She could hardly believe she was being so bold. The chemistry between them must be affecting her brain.

"I'll only go if you'll come, too." Humor sparkled in his eyes. She would have been at this meeting anyway.

"If you put it that way, how can I refuse?" Her lips tingled as he feathered one last kiss over them. She pulled herself away, slightly breathless, opened the door and went to get her laptop.

Everyone on the floor must know something by now. Or they'd figure it out from her burning cheeks. Or the loopy expression on her face.

And RJ had come right out and told Matthew! Did he plan to tell the entire family they were seeing each other? Surely the others would also worry about lawsuits. It hadn't occurred to her that she'd have a case against him, but her friend Evie had told her about a woman at her company who sued her boss when he dumped her. She'd won, even though it was consensual, because he was her direct boss and should not have embarked on a relationship with her.

It was easy to forget about all the pitfalls when she was in RJ's arms, or even gazing at his handsome face. The moment she moved away she felt exposed again to the chill winds of reality.

Brooke sat next to RJ during the meeting, which was normal since she sometimes needed to show him correspondence or data on her laptop. Opposite her, a tall blonde with a very large mouth was representing the Xingha Corporation, a manufacturer of children's toys that did a lot of business with U.S. supermarkets. Three non-English-speaking Chinese men in gray suits sat further along the table, and occasionally she turned to repeat something to them in Chinese.

"Oh, RJ, you must come to Beijing again soon. You'll love what they've done with your favorite hotel. Hot tubs in every room." Her dark eyes clashed with her blond hair, and gave her face a sense of drama that really annoyed Brooke. Already she found herself anxiously casting her mind back to RJ's trips to Beijing—had he even been to Beijing?—and wondering and worrying how intimate he'd been with Ms. Claudia Daring.

"I'm sure I'll be in Beijing sometime soon, but right now we have a lot happening here."

"I've heard." She leaned forward, and reached out to clasp his hands. "It's terrible. If there's anything I can do...anything at all."

Brooke barely managed not to roll her eyes, but

inside her stomach was churning. RJ and this woman had obviously had an affair.

She tried to glance sideways at RJ without moving her head. Were his eyes lighting up at the sight of Claudia's smile? He leaned back in his chair so she couldn't get a good look at him.

Matt sat farther down the table. What was he thinking about right now? Was he laughing at RJ being confronted with his own woman-loving ways at the first meeting of the day? She wished she could slide under the table and hide.

She was just the latest in a long line of Kincaid conquests. She knew that. You didn't work for RJ for five years and not realize that he enjoyed the company of women every bit as much as James Bond.

"You'll recall that we moved our account to Danmar Shipping in 2009 over pricing issues." Claudia lifted her rather pointy chin. "We understand you might be in a position to offer a more competitive price." One slender brow lifted slightly.

"Yes." Matthew chimed in from far down the table, although Claudia had addressed RJ. "We'd like to bring the Xingha Corporation back to The Kincaid Group, and we can provide some strong incentives. We understand that some of your new products are temperature sensitive and we can provide climate controlled..."

He continued speaking but Brooke no longer heard a word he said. She was staring directly at Claudia, who never took her eyes off RJ. Her breath caught as Claudia's tongue sneaked out and flicked over her upper lip. Probably supposed to look sensual, but it made Brooke think of a lizard.

Her eyes flew to RJ's face, and horror crept over her as she saw his familiar dimples deepen.

"Excuse me." She rose from her chair and hurried for the door, unable to contain herself for a single second longer. Once outside the meeting she walked quickly to the ladies' room. RJ was flirting with that woman, in front of everyone, when he'd slept with Brooke only yesterday!

And despite the fact that his brother knew about their affair and had taunted RJ for his womanizing ways not half an hour earlier.

Her breathing was rushed and unsteady and she wasn't surprised to see her face looking pale, except for a nasty flush spreading across her neck. That only happened when she was really embarrassed. How could she survive this meeting? If RJ had coolly rebuffed Ms. Daring, and perhaps said, "I'd love to come to Beijing, with my fiancée, Brooke Nichols," and gestured proudly toward her, she'd feel quite different.

"Ugh!" She said it aloud. This is what happened when you let your imagination run away with you. Even after RJ's conversation with Matt, she'd focused on the moment when he said it was unimaginable that he should tire of her, not the part where he had a new woman every week. Within an hour his dimples were deepening over some scrawny executive with an account to dangle.

Still, she had to go back. A bathroom break was one thing, ditching the meeting was another. And her laptop was still in there. She drew in an unsteady breath, patted cold water on her hot cheeks and dried it with a paper towel. *You're a professional and you can do this. You actually want The Kincaid Group to get this account because you care more about the future of the company than your future as RJ's latest female conquest.*

It wasn't working. Nevertheless, she gritted her teeth and strode out the door.

She plastered a smile on her face as she entered the meeting and sat down.

RJ turned to her. "Brooke, we came to an arrangement with Xingha, and we're going out for a celebration lunch. Can you book us a table at Montepeliano?"

"Sure." She maintained her stiff smile and picked up her phone. "How many people?" Was she invited or was she merely making reservations for RJ and his new bilingual playmate? She cursed the angry flames of jealousy that licked inside her. How had a few days of intimacy with RJ turned her into an irrational, emotional wreck?

"All of us." He glanced around the table. "Nine." A quick count revealed that did include her.

"Will do." She made the reservation in hushed tones. Great, now she had to sit through lunch watching Ms. Daring make eyes at RJ. And vice-versa. The restaurant was a short walk from the offices, and a favorite for business lunches.

"Do excuse us." RJ spoke to Claudia. "My assistant and I need a moment." He glanced at Brooke, and her heart jumped. Was he going to scold her for running out of the meeting? She was there to take minutes and she'd obviously missed the most important part—the deal. Of course Matt or RJ could fill her in on the details, but it was unprofessional of her to just vanish.

She followed him out of the room, and he gestured for her to come around the corner toward an empty conference room. Once inside, he closed the door. He looked at her and a tiny line appeared between his eyebrows.

"I'm sorry I left like that, I..." The rest of her words were lost when his mouth crushed over hers. His broad hands settled on her hips, and she shuddered, once, as his tongue slipped into her mouth.

Brooke heard a tiny moan leave her as the kiss deepened. Relief and the shock of excitement stirred her blood. Her nails scratched at RJ's strong back through his shirt, and she got a sudden urge to pull off his stiff suit jacket and feel his warm skin.

"Whoa, there." RJ pulled back, dimples deeper than ever. "Let's not get too carried away. The door's not even closed."

Brooke flushed. "Whoops."

"We'll use up all that energy later, and that's a promise." His blue eyes shone with dark fire. "Though it'll be hard to keep my hands off you for the rest of the afternoon. I guess this is why they say office romance is a bad idea."

"Just one of the reasons why it's a bad idea." A naughty smile crept across her mouth. "Makes it hard to stay focused in meetings, too."

"Or does the desire to get out of the meeting sharpen one's focus enough to make a deal in record time?"

"Yes, how did everything happen while I was in the washroom?"

RJ raised a brow. "I guess you'll never know." He gestured for her to leave the room before him, and she felt his fingers trail across her rear end as she turned to go. That sparked a little ripple of laughter. What did she care how they made the deal so fast? RJ had let her know he wanted her, not their glamorous client.

She walked to the restaurant on a cloud of joy. She didn't even mind RJ chatting with Claudia Daring. Now she had the perspective to see him using his charm to build the business, not to lure another woman into his bed. Her earlier flash of jealousy seemed petty and foolish.

She noticed Matthew casting wary glances at his brother. Was Matt worried she or RJ would somehow reveal their clandestine relationship? She knew the company couldn't afford even a wisp of scandal, so she made sure to sit at the far end of the table and did her best to make conversation with the Chinese men who had about twelve words of English among them.

That night she and RJ stayed at his place. His large, modern apartment had stunning views of the Charleston waterfront. They ordered in Thai curries and played a game of strip Go Fish then made lazy, intoxicating love on his oversize bed. After midnight they called a cab so she could go home, sleep and get ready for work.

By Thursday, at RJ's suggestion, she'd left a robe and a spare dress there, to avoid having to rush home. She took to carrying extra makeup and hair implements in her purse, because she now spent more time at his house than her own.

Her clothes looked strange hanging in the spare closet next to his off-season clothes. Of course if they lived together here, this would be her closet.

"I've decided to reinstitute a family tradition this week. Sunday gatherings at the old homestead."

"Your mom's house?"

She turned to see RJ frowning at the phone. "Yes. It may seem strange for us to go there when she's not in it, but she insists she wants us to get together and she'll be there in spirit. We've met for dinner nearly every Sunday since we were kids, and it doesn't feel right to drop the ball because everything's a mess right now. Besides, it'll be nice for you to meet the whole gang."

Her eyes widened. "Me? I don't know. Your family has a lot to talk about. And I don't want to scandalize them. They're sure to think it's odd that you're dating your assistant." Her stomach clenched as she immediately regretted the use of the word dating. That sounded so...serious, and RJ had plainly told Matt he had no idea where things were headed.

"Matt knows already."

She didn't plan to admit she'd heard Matt's reaction. "I don't want to be in the way."

"You won't be. My sister Lily will bring her new fiancé, Daniel, and Laurel—who you know—will bring her fiancé, Eli. Kara is planning both of their weddings. Then you already know Matt and you've probably met his fiancée, Susannah."

"Yes, I met her when she brought Flynn in to meet him for lunch." Flynn was Matt's toddler son, who'd recently scared everyone by getting some rare disease that had the family hovering over his bedside around the clock.

"Did you know Susannah is Flynn's mom?"

"But I thought Matt was married when... I mean, I know his wife passed away, but..." She felt her face heat. Matt's wife, Grace, had died in a small plane crash a year or so ago. Flynn must be just three, or thereabouts.

RJ laughed. "Matt didn't cheat on his wife. They'd hired her as a surrogate since Grace couldn't carry a child. What Grace and Matt never told us is that they used Susannah's egg, so Flynn was actually Susannah's biological child. She came back to Charleston in case he needed a compatible bone marrow donor when he was ill, and she and Matt fell in love. Pretty crazy, huh?"

"It's wonderful. For both of them and for Flynn."

"Romance is in the air amongst the Kincaids lately. It only seems fair that they get to know you, too."

"It would be nice to get to know your sisters. Sure, I'd love to come." Already caterpillars crawled in her stomach at the idea of them all looking at her. No doubt they would wonder why their brother was interested in someone ordinary like her.

"They'll love you." RJ crossed the bedroom and rested his hands on her hips. Her belly swirled with arousal. "And I know you'll love them, too."

I sure hope so. She sank into his embrace and enjoyed the warm, protected feeling of his arms around her. She was getting far too attached to RJ. Now she knew he was thoughtful, passionate and sexy as well as smart and gorgeous....

Brooke let out a small sigh. Everything was going so well. Somehow she'd climbed the tallest ladder on the chutes and ladders board and was sunning herself on a lofty square near the top. Why did she feel like a long chute was just around the corner?

Seven

Brooke agonized over what to bring to the meal, especially since she wasn't sure who the host was in Elizabeth Kincaid's absence. She didn't want to bring flowers and have them die alone in an empty house. She settled on a bottle of champagne and a hand-painted ceramic bowl filled with gourmet fudge.

She'd agreed to meet RJ there, and she felt a growing sense of trepidation as she walked past the other large, elegant mansions on tree-lined Montagu Street. As she approached the imposing Kincaid residence, she heard muffled voices through an open, lace-curtained window.

"You're kidding me!" A woman's voice. "Who invited him?"

"I did." Another female. "He's making a big effort to be a member of the family."

Brooke paused on the brick walkway to the front

door. Both voices were raised. She didn't want to enter into a scene.

"He's not even related to us. Alan is from Angela's second marriage."

"I invited Jack, too, but he didn't reply. Maybe he'll come anyway."

"Jesus, Kara. Why did you invite either of them? I just wanted a quiet family dinner, like we used to have." RJ's voice. His sister must have invited the sons of Reginald Kincaid's second family.

"I think we should give Alan a chance. He's been perfectly pleasant. He even seems interested in working for The Kincaid Group. Why not get to know him?" Brooke couldn't tell his sisters apart by their voices. She still hovered outside on the path, pretending to look for something in her purse.

"You always were too nice for your own good." RJ again. "At least Alan didn't inherit part of the company. He isn't even a relative. He's just an innocent bystander as far as this whole situation is concerned."

"Exactly. So let's welcome him into our midst. Anyone bring champagne?"

Brooke decided this was her cue, and she marched up the front steps and rang the bell. RJ greeted her with a warm kiss on the cheek and summoned her into a large, airy room with high ceilings and comfortable sofas. Everyone exclaimed over the champagne and fudge and she heaved a sigh of relief that she'd gotten off to a good start.

"This is my sister Lily." He gestured to a pretty woman with red-gold hair cascading over her shoulders. Her blue eyes were bright as she shook Brooke's hand.

"We've run into each other a few times at the office. Sometimes I hang around just to annoy RJ and Matt."

Matt, seated on a sofa with his toddler son on his lap, waved a cheery hello. She tried not to blush at the recollection of him discussing her with RJ.

"Daniel is Lily's fiancé," continued RJ. Brooke shook hands with a tall blond man with a warm smile. "And this is Kara. She's the event planner in the family."

"And right now I'm being blamed for overplanning this event." Her green eyes sparkled. "Trust me, people, I know what I'm doing."

RJ continued, "Of course you know Laurel." A striking beauty with long, auburn hair, Laurel Kincaid worked for the company as public relations director. She stepped forward and gave Brooke a kiss on the cheek, and introduced her fiancé, Eli, a tall, handsome man who Brooke knew owned a respected resort chain.

"We're glad you could come. It's nice to see RJ more relaxed lately." Laurel gave her brother a quick nudge.

"Brooke is definitely helping me keep things in perspective."

The doorbell rang again. The siblings looked at each other. "That must be Alan," whispered Laurel.

"I'll get it." Kara smiled and marched for the door. Brooke hadn't met either of the Sinclair men. She couldn't help a spark of curiosity at what the sons of Reginald Kincaid's former mistress would be like. All eyes swiveled to the door as Kara returned with a blondish man of medium height, smartly dressed in a wool jacket and pants.

RJ introduced her, and Alan Sinclair smiled and shook hands—firmly, Brooke noted—with everyone.

"Delighted to be here. So kind of you to invite me. What a stunning room!" He marveled over the crisp, Federal-era plasterwork.

Brooke had a feeling she'd seen him somewhere before. Maybe he'd come to the office for one reason or another. His hair curled just over his collar and gave him a raffish air, like a professor who slept with his students.

Now, now. You're as bad as the rest of them. Give him a chance. She didn't even know this man. She just knew RJ didn't want him here.

"Actually a lot of the details have been restored," Lily chimed in. "The house was a wreck when the family bought it. Dad's mother insisted on buying it and she spent years bringing back all the original features and furnishing it in period style."

"Which is why it looks more like a museum than a real house," murmured RJ.

"It is a museum, of sorts," Laurel spoke up. "A monument to an era that Grandma loved. She always wished she'd lived back in the 1800s, so she could swan around in long dresses and spend entire afternoons playing whist."

"She pretty much did that anyway," teased RJ. "Mom likes to have card parties, too. Mint juleps and cutthroat bridge."

There was a moment of silence, while they no doubt all thought of poor Elizabeth Kincaid sitting in the county jail.

Alan cleared his throat. "The house is obviously a labor of love. I don't suppose one of you would give me a tour?"

Laurel said, "Of course, I'd be happy to. Lily, is the meal under control?"

"Almost. Pamela should go away for the weekend more often. I love having the kitchen house to myself."

"Let me come help in the kitchen." Brooke was eager to make herself useful. In truth she was much happier working at an event rather than trying to make small talk, especially when they all must be wondering exactly why she was there.

She followed Lily outside into the manicured garden, and along a small brick walkway to the large, bright kitchen house. The building was a relic from the days when servants and their steamy labors could be kept separate from elegant family life, but had been renovated into a chef's kitchen with marble work tops and tall painted cabinets. Something delicious simmered in three pots on the stove and salad fixings sat, still bagged, on a long wooden table in the middle of the room. "Shall I make the salad?"

"That would be great. I'll just toast the garlic bread." Lily ripped off a hunk of French bread from one of three loaves and popped it in her mouth. "I'm in the second trimester of my pregnancy right now, and I'm absolutely ravenous."

"How exciting. Do you know if it's a boy or a girl?"

She pulled romaine lettuce from its bag and started to peel leaves off into a colander. "Not yet. We can't decide whether to find out. I know it's easier to know the gender because you can decorate the room, but I've also heard people can get really stressed about picking family names and creating expectations before the kid is even born. We went through a lot of drama just getting to this point, and I just want to enjoy our pregnancy without stirring up any more excitement."

Brooke rinsed the lettuce under a high, arched tap. "Having a baby must be one of the biggest adventures there is. You're bringing a brand-new person into your family, who you'll be spending the rest of your life with. It's magical, really."

Lily turned to her, eyes bright. "That's exactly how I feel. I admit I didn't intend to get pregnant, but it's brought Daniel and me closer than we would have dared become otherwise." She lowered her voice. "So are you and RJ...an item?"

"I guess we are." Brooke felt a little thrill of nerves. "Just since two weeks ago. I never intended for anything to happen, but..." She shrugged.

Lily's face turned more serious and her blue eyes looked steadily at Brooke. "Do be careful."

"What do you mean?" Brooke swallowed hard.

"Emotions are running high right now and the media's watching us all very closely."

Brooke's hands grew cold. "I'm not sure what you're saying."

Lily leaned in close. The lettuce dripped water onto the marble sideboard. "In case things don't work out between you, you know, it's important not to stir up any bad press."

"You think he'll break up with me and I'll go to the media?" First Matthew, now Lily. No doubt all the Kincaids suspected she'd betray the family. What would they say if they knew she'd told the police about their mom? Suddenly she felt like an intruder at their family gathering. If only she'd told RJ about it right away. Now there was so much water under the bridge she could hardly come out and admit her involvement. The deception by omission ate at her insides.

"No! None of us expects you to cause trouble." Lily put a hand on her arm. Her fingers felt soft, not accusatory. "I just want you to be prepared for anything and to handle it calmly. RJ's a smart, fun guy and a stand-up brother, but he's always sworn he'd never marry or have children." She gave a wry expression.

Brooke's stomach clenched. He'd actually said that? His own sister would know. And she was warning her to be careful not to get her heart broken. Brooke took the lettuce back to the wood table, and started to tear the leaves with shaking hands.

"I'd never deliberately stir up any trouble for the family," she said quietly. "I care very much about RJ, and about The Kincaid Group."

"I'm sure you do." Lily came close again. "I can see RJ looks different lately. More like his old self before Dad died. I'm sure that's attributable to you. I hope everything works out well."

Brooke heard the doubt in her voice. Brooke knew herself that RJ changed girlfriends like most men changed ringtones. She should be grateful for the wake-up call.

She and Lily chatted innocuously about a recent music festival, and Brooke prepared the rest of the salad, then they heard Alan's house tour coming toward the kitchen house.

"Stunning plasterwork in the archways." Alan's confident voice boomed outside the doorway. "She must have hired craftsmen from Italy."

"She did." Kara accompanied him into the room.

"Only the best for Grandma Kincaid. Do you ladies need some help with the food?"

"It's all ready." Lily smiled. "Perhaps you could both help us carry it into the dining room?"

The long mahogany table gleamed under its load of antique porcelain and sterling silver flatware. Obviously someone was polishing and dusting in Elizabeth Kincaid's absence. Not that she would clean things herself even if she was here.

Alan picked up one of the crystal glasses and peered underneath. "I knew it. Penrose Waterford. The original Waterford crystal." He beamed at the gathered group, taking their chairs. "It's a privilege to be surrounded by such treasures."

"It's fun to meet someone who appreciates them so much," said Laurel. "We tend to take everything for granted since we've seen all these things since we were babies." Little Flynn had picked up a scrolled silver spoon and raised it, ready to bang it down on the burnished wood surface before his father caught his hand with a laugh. "See! No appreciation for the finer things."

Alan laughed, showing even white teeth. "Born with a silver spoon in his mouth, lucky little devil. And surrounded by such a warm and loving family, too." He beamed at the gathered crowd.

Brooke shrank into her chair. He seemed perfectly comfortable here. She felt they were all watching her, wondering what would happen when RJ dumped her. RJ made such a handsome head of the family, carving the big roast and passing plates around. She helped herself to minted potatoes and steamed asparagus and raised her glass in a toast to the family and the fervent hope that Elizabeth Kincaid would be at next Sunday's gathering.

"What I want to know," said Matthew, "is who gave the police the information that led to Mom's arrest. They won't even say what the information is. The investigator RJ hired says someone saw Mom in the building, but the police aren't confirming."

Brooke's fingers tightened around her glass of white wine. She put it down carefully.

"Damn, but I wish I was there that night." RJ looked up. "I went out to a dinner across town and left around six, so I didn't see a thing."

Brooke swallowed, and stared at her asparagus. She'd been there until shortly after seven, finishing a report and PowerPoint presentation for one of RJ's upcoming meetings. That's when she'd joined Elizabeth Kincaid on the elevator and exited the building with her. Had RJ's mother been so upset because she'd found Reginald dead…or worse…killed him? No, no she couldn't believe it of her. Maybe she should just say something right now. She hadn't done anything wrong in speaking to the police, but sitting here in silence felt terrible. Perhaps she could just—

"If an employee told the police they saw Mom, they should be fired," RJ spoke loudly.

Brooke's knife rattled against her plate, and she cleared her throat and busied herself cutting some meat. Speaking up right now was not a good idea. She'd definitely have to tell RJ alone, not surprise him in front of his family. If only she could pluck up the courage.

"Be fair, RJ," Laurel said. "If they were just speaking the truth they've committed no crime. Mom did say she was there that night, bringing Dad's dinner."

"No way. It's a police investigation and they should have pled the fifth. It's a simple matter of company loyalty."

"Maybe they had no idea what was going on?" Lily peered at RJ over her glass of sparkling water.

"Hardly. The police were crawling all over the office for weeks investigating the murder. No one could have thought they were simply making casual conversation. Someone out there is responsible for our mother being behind bars right now, with a bunch of real hard cases and nut jobs, and that's not something I can forgive."

Brooke's breathing had become so shallow she started to feel faint. RJ would surely find out it was her who spoke to the police. Part of her wanted to confess right now and get it over with. Have them all shout at her and blame her and throw her out of the house. She silently twisted her napkin in her lap.

No, apparently she was too weak to speak up and face the music. And worst of all, she couldn't bear to hurt RJ.

And there was her job. And the rent to pay. And her dream of buying her little condo. She should probably start looking for another job, since they'd fire her for sure once they found out and it was bound to happen sooner or later.

"Brooke, are you okay? You look pale?" Kara turned to her.

"Sure, fine!" Her voice came out loud and forced. "Delicious dinner." Her lame comment echoed down the table.

"Marvelous." Alan smiled and lifted his knife.

"Quite the most succulent roast I've had this year. My congratulations to the chef."

Lily smiled. "Mom taught me everything I know. She's an amazing entertainer. Speaking of which, Laurel, she wanted to know how your wedding plans are coming along. Did you choose the dress yet?"

Laurel looked slightly startled. "Choose a dress? I can't possibly get married until Mom is out of…that place."

"She wants us to forge ahead with all our plans so she can leap right back into life once this ordeal is over. She and I spent ages poring over menu ideas for my wedding. And she thinks I should go for the Vera Wang dress I showed you."

Laurel bit her lip. "I don't know. It just seems wrong to think about dresses and cakes and reception venues at a time like this." She turned to Eli. "Don't you think?"

"Absolutely." He patted her hand. "No need to rush. We have the rest of our lives together."

"I agree with Mom and think you're being silly. Come on, Eli. Don't you think Mom would be cheered up by pictures of your lovely bride in sixty or seventy different fabulous gowns?" Eli shrugged in response to Kara's question. "I tell you, I'm more excited about this wedding than the bride or groom. If they didn't have a party planner in the family, there probably wouldn't ever be a wedding.

"I think everyone needs a party planner in the family. Come on, I'm up to three weddings right now, Lily and Daniel, Matt and Susannah, Laurel and Eli—who's next?"

Brooke felt a sudden raw flush of irrational hope in her chest. Why not her and RJ?

Well, there were any number of reasons why not. RJ didn't say anything and she forced herself not to look at him. Lily's warning reverberated in her mind.

"Alan, how about you? Have you got a blushing bride hidden somewhere?"

"Not yet, I'm afraid." He smiled around the table. "I'm still waiting for that perfect lady to enter my life." Brooke noticed his eyes skip right past her as he shone his klieg-light charm on the gathered group. He probably wasn't interested in her since she wasn't a member of the mighty Kincaid family. She was just a nobody who happened to be there. "And who knows, it could happen any day now." He let his blue eyes fall to rest on Kara, and Brooke watched the slight suggestive lift of his eyebrow.

"That's the spirit." Kara smiled. Then she clapped her hand over Eli's. "I still think you should be pushing your bride to make some decisions. One couple I helped recently had been engaged for sixteen years. They hadn't planned it that way, they just never got around to setting the date."

"Maybe they just weren't all that crazy about each other." RJ topped up the glasses of those seated on either side of him. "When people realize that they really like each other, things happen fast." His bright gaze settled on Brooke, who couldn't stop a smile rushing to her lips.

"Maybe you'll be next then, RJ?" Kara looked at him with an arch smile.

RJ laughed. "Or maybe you will, Kara?"

Brooke deflated as suddenly as she'd filled with

hope. Which was absolutely ridiculous after two measly weeks of dating. You'd think she'd never been in a relationship before.

"Since I'm not even seeing anyone right now, I'm not entirely sure how that could happen." Kara took the bottle from him and refilled the next two glasses down the table. "But I suppose you never know what life is going to bring."

"Truer words were never said." Alan beamed around the room. "I never imagined I'd find myself in the midst of such a charming family. I'm honored to be here and delighted to find that I truly feel at home among you."

Brooke wished she could say the same. But, kind as they were, she still felt like an outsider. The kind of outsider who was responsible for putting their beloved mother behind bars. And when they found out, she'd be on the outside for good.

Eight

"I guess Alan's not so bad after all." RJ piloted his Porsche back to his apartment. Brooke sat beside him, looking gorgeous in a green dress that gracefully hugged her curves.

"He's certainly making an effort." Brooke seemed a little tense, her pretty mouth tight and her lovely green eyes darting around a lot. He'd be sure to release all that tension with a nice, soothing massage when they got home. His fingers tingled with anticipation at the prospect.

"Was it overwhelming being surrounded by Kincaids?"

"Everyone in your family is lovely. They couldn't have been nicer."

"Still, there are a lot of us. And more all the time, it seems. The clan keeps growing." He beamed. He loved the way she'd pitched in with Sunday dinner and he could tell she'd made a positive impression on his sisters. "You fit right in." There weren't many women as intelligent and fun as his sisters, but he'd managed to find one. That she was gorgeous, too? Icing on the cake.

"Thanks. I've had practice, being in the company so long, I knew half of you already."

"But socializing is different. For one thing you look a lot hotter in that dress than in your power suits." How could he not have noticed how breathtakingly beautiful she was until recently? He must have been blind. He took the briefest of red-light opportunities to admire the way her dress draped over her slender thighs, and saw her smile out of the corner of his eye.

"Thanks."

"I can't wait to peel it off you."

"You won't have to wait long."

He pulled into the parking garage under his building and they hurried upstairs, laughing at their own eagerness. Every glance, every touch that passed between them only ratcheted the tension higher. RJ's muscles ached to wrap themselves around Brooke again. He'd made an effort not to paw her in front of the family, as he didn't want to embarrass her. He could tell she still felt a little shy and awkward, probably because she was used to having a much more formal relationship with all of them.

In the elevator, RJ seized the opportunity to steal a greedy kiss. Brooke's mouth tasted like honey and flowers, and her skin was smooth silk under his fingers. How could he have worked with her for five years and never realized such a delicious and inviting woman was right under his nose?

So much for being sensible and keeping work and play separate for five years. If it hadn't been for that one crazy whisky-fueled night he could have missed out on becoming intimate with the most appealing woman he'd ever met.

They tore into the apartment, flushed and breathless. Brooke fumbled with the buttons on his shirt while he unwrapped the complicated sash around her waist. Her nipples poked eagerly through the delicate fabric of her bra when he unzipped her dress and let it fall to the floor.

He circled her waist and held her against his chest. Brooke let out a shuddering sigh. He could tell she'd been anxious today, maybe nervous about making the right impression on his large family. Now they were alone again her reserve melted away, leaving her warm and eager in his arms.

Their kisses had a dimension he'd never experienced before. Something more than taste and touch, a thrilling quality that never failed to surprise him. Her mouth fit his so well, he could kiss her for hours and not notice the time passing.

Brooke's hand covered his erection through the pants they'd not yet managed to shed, and he released a little groan of his own.

"I feel like a teenager when you're around." He breathed in her ear and nibbled the nape of her neck. "I had a hard time keeping my hands off you today."

"Lucky thing you don't have to anymore." She stroked the hard length of him, then unzipped his pants and took him firmly in her hand. RJ arched his back at the sensation.

"I think we'd better get horizontal."

Brooke squeezed again, making him breathe harder.

"Horizontal is so...predictable." She spoke quietly. He cracked open his eyes to see her mischievous grin.

"Brooke, you never fail to surprise me." They shrugged off his pants and he lifted her onto the back of the broad leather sofa, which was just wide enough to hold her gorgeous ass while he held her steady.

It drove him crazy to see how wet and ready she was. He entered her slowly, and enjoyed her sweet moan of pleasure. Her breasts bounced gently against his chest as he rocked back and forth. He loved the feel of her hands on his back, clinging for balance as he moved with her. When she wrapped her legs around his hips and pulled him deeper, he thought he'd explode right there and then, but he pulled himself back from the brink and teased her lips with licks and kisses.

"Oh, RJ." His name on her sigh heightened his arousal. He sensed her climax growing close. Her nails dug into his skin and she moved with increasing speed and passion, legs still wrapped firmly around him. When she finally let go, he felt the force of serious relief ripping through him, and they almost toppled backwards onto the sofa together until he managed to right them.

Still in the same position, he picked her up and carried her into the bedroom, where they settled on the bed. Brooke's eyes were closed, her lashes long and thick against her rosy cheeks. Her hair splayed over the pillow and her lips were red and slightly parted.

"What a vision," he murmured.

Her eyes opened a little, a sliver of jade green glory, and he saw the spark of a smile in them. Brooke's smile did something really odd to his chest. In fact he was currently experiencing a host of unfamiliar sensations. Is this what love felt like?

He settled next to her onto the pillow. Brooke had already drifted off into a sweet sleep, and he was almost ready to do the same until he realized he'd better go remove the condom.

Which was when he realized he hadn't used one.

Brooke woke up to the first rays of lazy sunshine peeking around the heavy curtains. She'd slept like a corpse. The anxiety of the family dinner knocked her right out. Or maybe her brain was hiding from the ugly reality of the truths she had to reveal. She turned to find RJ, but his side of the bed was empty.

When she glanced at the clock it was only 6:30. Early for him to be up already.

"RJ?" How odd. He didn't seem to be in the bathroom, and the bedroom door was closed. She tried to settle her head back on the pillow, but found she couldn't relax. She climbed out of bed and pulled her robe from the wardrobe, then stepped out into the living room.

Still no RJ.

The kitchen was empty, and so was the spare bedroom. The door to his office was closed. Not exactly an early riser, RJ usually rolled out of bed at the last minute when it was time to head to work. She'd never known him to work in his study in the morning. Maybe something was going on with his mother's case?

That now-familiar knot of fear reappeared in her stomach. Had he realized it was her who spoke to the police?

"RJ, are you in there?"

She heard a rustle, and the sound of a chair being pulled back, then the door flung open. RJ's face was dark, his eyebrows lowered.

Immediately Brooke felt the blood creeping from her body. He knew. "I'm sorry, I never meant to—"

"Don't blame yourself. I screwed up, Brooke."

"What?" She was confused.

RJ shoved a hand through already disordered hair. "I've been taking responsibility for birth control, so it's my fault I forgot to use a condom."

Brooke's mouth fell open. She'd been so excited and aroused it never crossed her mind. "I didn't even think of it."

"You could be pregnant."

The words hung in the air for a moment. Her hand flew to her belly as if life was already taking shape in there. Which it might be.

"I can't believe I was so stupid." RJ's tone made it clear there was nothing positive about the possibility.

Brooke shrank back into the living room slightly. For an odd, irrational second, she'd welcomed the idea of RJ's baby. Now she could plainly see he was horrified by the possibility of having a child with her. "It was my fault, too. I should have said something."

"It's not your fault. I've taken care of it every time, so you could reasonably expect me to continue." He hesitated. "I don't suppose you're on the pill or anything, are you?"

She swallowed. "No. I should have gone to the doctor for something, but everything happened so fast…." Their whirlwind romance had seemed above prosaic matters like birth control. And the sad fact was she hadn't had a relationship in so long that she hadn't thought about contraception in ages. She had an old diaphragm buried somewhere in her bathroom cupboards, but it probably didn't even fit anymore.

RJ shook his head. "With everything that's going on, the last thing we need is more worry. And considering that our current situation was precipitated by my dad's illegitimate son, you'd think I'd be more careful." He wasn't looking at her, but right past her, into the living room.

Our child wouldn't be illegitimate if you married me. The thought penetrated her brain before she had a chance to stop it. The man right in front of her looked like he had no intention of marrying anyone, ever. Just as his sister had warned her.

"How soon will we know?" He turned his gaze back to her, where it hit her like a blow.

"Uh, I think it's at least a month." Didn't you have to miss a period, or something? She'd never been in a position to worry about it before. Her periods were as regular as tax bills. She hugged her robe about her. The mood had morphed from fevered excitement to worry and regret. "I guess I should get ready for work." Where she'd be sitting outside his office all day, knowing he was in there wishing he'd never met her and hoping and praying that she wasn't pregnant with his child.

The reality of the situation settled like a stone in her stomach.

"I'm sorry, Brooke." The pain in his blue eyes scratched a tiny hole in her soul. She wanted to say, "Don't worry about it," or something equally banal, but RJ's grim countenance made her keep her platitudes to herself. She turned and walked back to the bedroom, each footstep feeling like a mile. She managed to shower and climb into the clean suit she'd left there. Her eyes looked hollow as she brushed her teeth at RJ's sink. She'd been tiptoeing along, enjoying her romance with RJ and skirting all conflict for as long as she could. She'd finally hit that game board chute she'd worried about, and now she'd landed in a heap back at the bottom of the board, sitting on a pile of shattered dreams with an aching heart.

"Oh, Brooke, I won't say I told you so." Evie sat opposite Brooke on the sofa in her living room, sympathy in her big brown eyes and her freshly made martini sitting un-sipped in her hand. "But I had a feeling something like this would happen. I've never heard of anyone having an affair with the boss and going on to enjoy decades of happy marriage afterwards."

Brooke put her own martini down on the coffee table. Making it had been a welcome distraction, but she didn't have the heart to drink it. Besides, alcohol might make her more emotional, which was definitely not a good thing right now. And there was the possibility that she might be pregnant, which meant she shouldn't be drinking at all. "Trust me, I know! I never intended to have an affair with him. It just happened. I knew it wasn't a good idea from the moment we first kissed, but it was so..." She groped around her brain for words.

Perfect...magical...dreamy...wonderful...sensual... amazing...

She didn't feel like voicing any of those out loud right now.

"I've told you before that I see a pattern in your relationships." Evie drew her brows together slightly, the way she did when she was about to get serious.

"What relationships? I haven't had a date in over a year."

"Is it that long? Well, you did say you wanted to take a break. And I don't blame you, after the blond guy."

"Sam." Brooke grimaced slightly. "He seemed sweet at first."

"He seemed needy." Evie sipped her drink. "He was needy. I think that's why you were drawn to him. He wanted someone to tell all his problems to, a shoulder to cry on and someone to have lots of warm sympathy sex with."

Brooke chuckled. "Not lots of sex. Trust me."

"And that guy you dated in college, Ricky. He was seriously high maintenance. I'm not sure how you managed to attend your classes and hold a job while tending to his many needs."

"RJ's not needy. He's extremely capable, independent, brilliant...."

"And going through the biggest personal crisis of his life. At any other time he'd probably be a different person, but in the last few weeks he's been a strapping, muscular bag of needs, and you've been doing your best to meet them all."

"You are right about the strapping and muscular part." A tiny smile tugged at her lips. Then she wiped it away. "I was crazy about RJ for years. Long before all this latest drama. I can't believe I forgot all about contraception and gave him yet another thing to worry about. If only I could turn back the clock and—"

"Stop trying to save everybody."

"My desire to save everybody may be what makes me such a good executive assistant."

"Then stop doing it at work, too. I thought you wanted to move into management."

Brooke stared at her untouched martini. "I hope I still have a job to go to. If RJ gets tired of dating me he's not going to want to see my face every day."

"So, apply for another job before it happens. Didn't you say the HR lady thought you had potential for promotion?"

"I think she was just trying to let me down easy when I got passed over for the Events job. She did tell me to come back and try again, though. She almost hinted that RJ wasn't willing to give me up just yet."

"What?" Evie sat up. "Did you ask him about it?"

"No." Brooke sighed. "I never even told him I'd applied. I thought it would be awkward if I got rejected."

"You'd better believe he knew about it. His family owns the company." Evie raised a brow. "They'd better not try any funny business, especially if you're pregnant. Then you'll really need the job."

"I know." Brooke hugged herself. "I've heard pregnant women can't even get health insurance these days unless it's through an employer."

"Don't panic yet. You don't even know if you are pregnant." Evie leaned forwards and rested her chin on tented hands. "Would you marry him?"

Brooke shrank under her inquiring stare. "You mean if I was pregnant?"

"Yes, and he decided to be a gentleman and face up to his responsibilities."

Brooke pulled further back into her chair. "Not if it was an obligation for him." What a horrible thought.

That RJ might feel compelled to marry her out of duty. "I'd hate that."

Not that he'd seemed at all inclined to propose this morning. His grim expression still haunted her mind, and he'd managed to be out of the office most of the day in "meetings" that weren't on the calendar. They'd made no more after-work plans.

Maybe this was the end?

Perhaps he'd simply grow more distant and there'd be no more mention of kisses or weekends in the mountains. They'd go back to sharing memos and emails, rather than hugs and sly glances.

Her hands grew cold just thinking about it.

Or worse, maybe he'd want her out of sight. She might get transferred to a "crucial position" at the dockyard, or maybe even one of the overseas offices. She'd lose her job—and her health insurance—just when she needed them most.

"Don't look so grim." Evie tapped her hand, drawing her back into the present. "No one's died yet!"

"Except RJ's father."

Evie grimaced. "I forgot. Poor RJ, he really does have it coming at him from all angles. Do they still think his mom did it?"

"Apparently so. She's still being held without bail."

"I bet if you could spring her you'd make him the happiest man alive."

"I'd love to, but that would mean knowing who murdered his dad." She didn't want to admit, even to Evie, that she was the person responsible for his mom being arrested. "Apparently there's a paper log kept at the security desk of everyone who enters and leaves the building, but the page for that day is missing."

"The killer must have taken it."

"I'd imagine so." The killer had been in the building with her that night. She suppressed a shiver. "It's scary knowing there's someone out there who could kill Reginald Kincaid in cold blood."

"And no one knows why."

"That's the weirdest part. I know RJ has suspicions about Reginald's oldest son, Jack, who he left a huge stake in the company to. He keeps his distance from the rest of the family, almost as if he has something to hide."

"Sounds very guilty."

"But apparently Reginald knew, or at least suspected, that someone was out to get him. He wrote letters to all the family members, to be read in the event of his death. If he suspected his son Jack, why would he leave him almost half his company?"

"Maybe it was RJ?" Evie lifted a brow. Humor glittered in her eyes, which was enough to prevent Brooke getting upset.

"Yes, and maybe he'll kill me next so I won't sue him for sexual harassment. His brother Matthew actually warned him I might do that."

"Would you?" Evie's eyes widened.

"Never. It was utterly consensual so I'd be a real loser if I sued."

"Might be easier than winning the lottery, though."

"I'd rather take my chances with the Powerball."

"I notice how you deftly dodged my question about RJ being the murderer. Just for the sake of argument, he does have motive. Maybe he found out about his dad's second family and was so mad he wanted revenge?"

Brooke shook her head. "That's not his style. He's too smart to risk spending his life in prison, for one thing. And he really loved his dad. It's easy to see. He told me about all the time they spent together at their cabin in the woods, and how much he misses him every day." Her heart filled with emotion just thinking about the look in his eyes when he spoke of his father.

"Shame, because discovering he's a killer would really help you go off him if things turn sour."

"Maybe this crisis will help us grow together."

"See, there you go again, looking for troubled waters to pour oil on. You need to find a nice, uncomplicated guy without a care in the world," Evie said.

"Except that I'm in love with RJ." She said it aloud, needing to admit it to her best friend as well as herself. The word *love* gave her a rush as it sounded in the air of her condo. "I truly am."

"I can tell." Evie tilted her head and gave Brooke a sympathetic look. "Go on. Call him. You know you want to." She looked at Brooke's phone where it sat on the coffee table next to her keys.

A rush of adrenaline prickled Brooke's fingers and toes. Did she dare? Maybe he'd be thrilled to hear from her and tell her to come on over. Then they could spend the night making love in his big bed and share a sleepy breakfast in their robes before walking to work together.

She picked up the phone and dialed his number.

"Who?" RJ stood up violently from his chair and shoved his hand through his hair. Matt was in his office, along with Laurel and corporate investigator Nikki Thomas. Tall, with shoulder-length black hair and blunt bangs that framed intense blue eyes, Nikki had found the private investigator RJ had hired to look into the murder. Tony Ramos, a tall man with a shaved head and a way of making you feel he could read every thought in your head. "We all know someone saw Mom here on the night of the murder. She told me so herself, but who the hell was it and why won't anyone tell me?"

"Yeah, who was it?" Matt paced in front of the door. They were all on edge, as the D.A.'s office had just turned down their umpteenth request for bail.

"Brooke Nichols."

The name fell like a stone in the crowded office. All eyes swiveled to RJ.

"You're kidding me." He looked from Matt to Laurel. Everyone in the room seemed frozen to the spot. He felt his head begin to pound. "It couldn't be Brooke. She would have said something."

Laurel swallowed, and Matt looked down at the carpet.

"You got this information from the police?" Anger and confusion rose and snarled in his chest. His phone started vibrating in his pocket, and he reached in to turn it off.

Ramos nodded. "Yes. They interviewed all the employees the next day, and there were only five people in the building after seven that evening. Unfortunately security only had people sign in on a paper log, and—as we all know—it went missing. These are the people who admitted to being there, and Jimmy, the security guard who was on duty that night, said these are also the only people he remembers seeing. Alex Woods, the night shipping clerk, Reginald himself, his wife, Elizabeth, and Brooke Nichols."

RJ blew out a hard breath. Brooke, the person he trusted more than anyone else in the world, had kept this from him. "Why didn't she tell me?"

"Maybe because she was afraid you'd react like this?" Laurel raised a brow. "All she did was tell the truth, RJ. Would you have wanted her to lie?"

"None of the others saw Mom?"

"Jimmy says she waved hello. Nothing out of the ordinary. Apparently Brooke later told the investigating officer Mrs. Kincaid seemed anxious, or stressed."

"Dammit." RJ banged his fist on the desk. "Poor Mom stuck in that place with all those criminals because of a thoughtless comment. Brooke couldn't possibly suspect Mom."

"I'm sure she doesn't, RJ." Matt rubbed his eyes. "This situation is a giant quicksand swamp that everyone is getting sucked into. What we need is to find the real killer. Any news on that, Tony?"

"The police have eliminated all the other people who were here from their inquiries, and I admit I've done the same. The only possibility is an intruder no one saw."

"We have security on the desk 24/7," said RJ. "We're in a competitive business, and shipping containers can hold a lifetime's worth of trouble so we're ultra conscious of who comes and goes from this building and all our other facilities. Everyone has to come through the lobby. There's no other way into the building."

The investigator narrowed his sharp eyes. "I've checked all the windows and the former cargo doors that were sealed shut. The building is as tight as one of your container ships. The assailant could only have come through the lobby. He also must have removed the log page at some point. Jimmy says the only time the desk is left unattended is when he goes to the bathroom. He said he always bolts the lobby doors before leaving the desk, and he's sure he did so that night." Tony looked from Laurel to RJ. "But when he came back from the can and went to unlock the door, the bolt was pulled."

"So someone left the building while he was in the bathroom." Laurel's hand flew to her mouth. "And it wasn't Mom because Jimmy said she left much earlier."

"Exactly," Nikki chimed in. "The big snag is, other than Jimmy's word, there's no concrete proof of when she left the building, and even if there was proof, she came and left right around the time of the murder."

"When did Brooke leave?" RJ's gut churned. He hated that she was now involved in this mess. His fury at her deception was tempered by worry that she'd be somehow implicated.

"She left at the same time as your mother. They came down in the elevator together. Apparently Brooke got on the elevator as Mrs. Kincaid came down from visiting your dad's office."

"But Brooke isn't a suspect."

"Nope. Never was."

RJ felt a small wave of relief. Then his head started to ache again when he wondered why she'd never told him any of this. They'd been intimate in every way. He'd shared stories about his dad that he'd never told anyone, and she never mentioned that she'd said anything to the police. Her behavior was bizarre and troubling, especially since the subject had been discussed openly with her in the room, including at the family dinner. Why had she kept such crucial information from him?

And what if she was pregnant, right now, with his baby? Choosing to have a baby was a huge, lifetime responsibility that should grow from careful thought and planning, not spring from a steamy night of sex. The situation was further complicated by him being her boss. At this point, that was a nightmare. He couldn't keep a straight face while she walked in and out of his office with letters and files, acting like everything was completely normal and they'd never done more than hold hands.

"RJ, are you still with us?"

"What?" He realized Matt had been talking to him.

"Tony wants to know if he should talk to Brooke, hear exactly what she told the police."

"No. I'll talk to her myself." He'd avoided her all day, wary of the effect her big green eyes had on him, but there was no avoiding the conversation they needed to have right now.

He tried hard to tug his attention back to the reason for this meeting. "We need to find out more about the suspected intruder. Has the building been combed for fingerprints?"

Tony shrugged. "This office building is fifty years old. There are tens of thousands of fingerprints on every surface."

"Dad redecorated his office not long ago." Laurel spoke up. "And surely the killer was in there."

"The police went over the office during the initial investigation. I'll talk to them about our new theory of a separate intruder who hid in the building and see what they have." Tony typed something into his laptop.

"Jack Sinclair is still top of my list." RJ looked from Tony to Nikki. "And now apparently he's spreading the word that he plans to use his new shares to make changes in the company. Nikki, didn't you say his car was parked in a nearby lot on the night of the murder?"

"Uh, I'm not sure it was his car. The police are still looking into it."

"You can use your skills to dig into his corporate activities and see if he's been working to damage our company."

"I'm not sure why he'd do that when he's the biggest shareholder."

"Am I sensing reluctance?" RJ frowned at her. Why did she keep finding excuses not to dig up dirt on Jack?

Nikki blinked and tucked a neat lock of black hair behind her ear. "Of course not. I'll look into the situation from all my usual angles. I'll report back as soon as I find anything."

RJ nodded. "And I'll talk to Brooke and see if she remembers anything else about that night." If he knew she was there he'd have asked her earlier. Even the tiniest shred of evidence in the right direction could get his mom out of jail, which was the most important thing right now.

More important than his affair with Brooke. When he was with Brooke, everything else faded into the background. He forgot about his responsibilities and worries. He needed to pull off the rose-tinted glasses and find out exactly what was going on in that sharp mind of hers. How could she have been so thoughtless?

When the others had left his office he pulled out his

phone and saw the call he missed was from Brooke. He pressed the button to return the call, and as soon as she picked up he said, "I'm coming over."

Nine

No amount of sun salutations could calm Brooke down after RJ's brusque phone call. He'd told her he'd be there in twenty minutes, then hung up. She rolled up her yoga mat and put it in the closet, then commenced to wiping down her kitchen countertops—again—like someone with obsessive-compulsive disorder.

She jumped a good few inches when she heard a loud knock on the door.

"Coming." She tried to steady her breathing as she pulled the latch.

RJ's fierce blue gaze hit her like a blast of icy air. He walked into the room, as tall and erect as a statue.

She closed the door. *Hi, RJ. How are you doing? Did you have a good day?* Normal pleasantries stuck in her throat.

"You told the police you saw my mother on the night

of the murder." He spoke quietly, but his voice held an edge of steel.

"Yes, I did." She managed to keep her voice from shaking. "I never suspected her, but I did see her as I was leaving, and when they asked me, I simply told them."

"Your testimony is the reason she's being held without bail. You're the reason they consider her a suspect."

She felt herself shrink under his gaze. "All I said was that she was in the elevator when it stopped on our floor, carrying a large bag."

"With dinner for my dad."

"I didn't know what was in the bag."

"You said she seemed...distressed." His eyes narrowed. She fought the urge to step back, away from the force of his fury.

"She had tears in her eyes, or the beginning of tears. And she looked anxious. I think that's what I said. It's hard to remember, it was weeks ago." She felt tears rise in her own eyes. "I never imagined they'd arrest her."

"You knew the police were investigating a murder and looking for suspects." His gaze bored into her.

"Yes." She swallowed. "All I did was tell them the truth."

"Why didn't you say anything to me? We've all been wondering why they're holding Mom without bail, and it's because of your testimony."

"Why?" She blinked back the tears that still threatened. "I suppose I knew you'd be angry."

His eyes flashed with a mix of anger and confusion. "I'm not angry that you spoke the truth, but for you to keep it secret all this time, while we were together and so intimate." He shook his head. "I don't understand it and it makes me feel like I don't know you, Brooke."

She took a step back, shrinking under the force of his stare. "I'm truly sorry I didn't say anything. I wanted to but the time never seemed right and then it was weird that I hadn't already told you." She hadn't wanted to mess up their budding romance. That seemed to have gone right down the toilet. She'd better hope nothing resulted from their little mistake last night. A thick, heavy sadness descended over her.

"Why didn't you tell me my mom looked upset? Don't you think I'd want to know?"

"I didn't see you until the next day when we all arrived to the news that your dad was dead. I never got a chance to talk to you in private until after the police interviewed me." She shivered slightly, remembering that terrible day. Yellow crime scene tape in Reginald's office, swarms of investigators everywhere, press jamming the doorway to the building.

"So you were one of the last people in the building before the murder."

She nodded. "I wish I could be more help in finding out who did it."

"Maybe you can." He rubbed his temples. "Did you notice anything unusual?"

She hesitated. "Your mother being there was unusual. I don't remember her bringing him dinner too often."

His eyes narrowed. "You do suspect her, don't you?"

"No, I'm just answering your question." She lifted her chin. She'd tried to do the right thing. It didn't occur to her at the time that her few words would lead to an arrest.

"She said she and Dad had an argument the night before, and he left for work in a mood, then called saying he'd be working late, so she decided to soften him up by bringing his favorite roast beef and potatoes." RJ crossed his arms. "Not exactly suspicious."

Brooke kept her mouth closed. She could see why the police were suspicious, especially given all the information about Reginald's infidelity that came to light after his death. She hadn't known about any of that when she spoke to the police.

The corner lamp in her living room threw RJ's strong features into high relief. Why did he have to be so handsome? Her life would be so much easier if her boss was a balding, middle-aged guy with a potbelly. Even now, with tension hardening the lines of his face and darkening his blue eyes, he was stunning. And the way he leaped in to defend his mom only showed what a loyal family man he was.

Her heart ached. "I so wish I'd seen someone else, or noticed anything strange. I've gone over that evening so many times in my head, but it was just a regular day in so many ways, until we discovered what happened."

"My dad was murdered within minutes of you leaving. The killer must have been in the building."

"What does your mom say? Did she see anyone?"

He shook his head. "No one. She said she went to Dad's office and the door was closed, so she knocked. He didn't answer, so she opened the door and he was sitting at his desk. He told her to go away."

"What?" She'd never heard Reginald speak that way to anyone.

"Yup. Nice, huh? She was totally shocked. She told him she brought dinner and he said he didn't want any and for her to go home, now. She said he almost growled it at her."

"That's terrible."

"And that's her last memory of my dad. Now she's in jail for killing him. And you just *forgot* to tell me you shared the elevator with her that night."

She lowered her eyes. "I'm so sorry, RJ."

"We need to take a break from each other. I'd like you to take a paid leave of absence, starting immediately." She glanced up, to see his brows lowered in a frown. "In fact, I'll double your pay if you'll stay home until things clear up around here."

Brooke's knees went weak. Did this mean she was fired? She'd already figured out that her relationship with RJ was over.

"Tasha can take over your duties in the meantime. If there's anything personal at the office, I'll have her send it here."

She felt like she'd been slapped. RJ's pained expression tugged at her heart and she wanted to reach out to him and say she never meant to hurt his mom, but he wanted her to vanish.

"I'll get my laptop. Tasha will need it." Her voice barely rose above a whisper. She tried her best to keep tears out of her voice. She moved to her work bag, which was near the kitchen table, and fished out her laptop. Her hand trembled as she handed it to RJ. Her fingers brushed his thumb as he took it from her and she steeled herself against the jolt of energy that passed between them.

Last night she'd lain in his bed. Tonight she'd sleep here alone.

RJ was already at the door. "Your increased pay will

be wired directly into your account. You will not return to work until further notice." He avoided her gaze. He hesitated with his hand on the door handle. "But if you learn of anything…unexpected…"

Her mind flew to his reaction this morning when he realized they forgot to use a condom.

"I'll call you if anything important happens." Her voice sounded so tiny, like it was coming from far away.

RJ turned one time to look at her, eyes hooded and face set in a hard line, then he tugged open the door, stepped out and closed it firmly behind him.

Brooke collapsed onto the sofa, and the tears flowed like summer rain. This beat all the bad outcomes she'd imagined for their relationship. Obviously she hadn't been creative enough in imagining how things could go wrong. He'd literally ordered her to keep away from him, and was paying her twice her salary to stay out of his sight.

She hugged herself, suddenly cold. If only she'd told him sooner about her encounter with his mother. He might still have been annoyed that she told the police, but he could hardly blame her. Her secrecy, however—born of cowardice—was inexcusable. She knew that. His anger was justified, and seared her like a hot brand.

RJ slammed the door of his Porsche and fired up the engine. His entire body was on fire with rage and hurt. Brooke had been his port in this crazy ongoing tempest, and all the time he'd held her, and lain with her and kissed her, she'd neglected to tell him that she had identified his mom at the scene of his father's murder.

You really couldn't ever know people. His father's

untimely passing and the wake of chaos it left behind should have hammered that home. Everyone had secrets that grew and tangled like briars, snaring them in a web of deception.

He roared through the streets, wishing he could drive fast enough to blow right out of this dimension into another life where none of this was happening.

He wanted to go visit his mom, but he hadn't obtained special permission to see her in person and the thought of talking to her via a video monitor made his chest hurt. It was past visiting hours anyway.

He swung into the underground parking of his building and pulled into his space. For a moment he rested his head and hands on the wheel. How could he face going back to his empty apartment when only last night he and Brooke had shared such a joyful night? At least until he realized how his foolish mistake could have ruined everything. The last thing any of them needed at a time like this was an unexpected pregnancy.

He hauled himself out of the car and took the elevator up to his apartment. As expected the large space seemed chill and empty. He'd barely even been there without Brooke for the last couple of weeks. They'd grown so used to each other's company that it seemed stranger for them to be apart than together.

The answering machine light flashed green, so he walked over and pressed the button. "RJ, it's Lily. Mom's been released! The lobby door being unbolted from the inside late at night was enough to make her eligible for bail. She's on her way home right now. Come over and join us for a celebration."

"Yes!" RJ did a fist pump. "About time." He picked up the phone and dialed Lily. "I'll be right there."

Glad to leave the lonely space of his apartment, he almost ran back to the elevator. It was as quick to walk to the family mansion as to drive, so he set off along Charleston's familiar streets with renewed vigor. Despite everything that had happened with Brooke, his heart soared with relief that his mom was out of that grim place, back in her beloved home.

Her body felt frail and thin when he hugged her in the front hallway of her house. "I'm desperate to style my hair." She patted her dark hair self-consciously. "My gray roots were previously a secret between my hairdresser and myself. I'll have to see if he can squeeze me in first thing tomorrow." Her soft, old-Charleston lilt was music to his ears.

"I can see you have your priorities straight, Mom." Kara squeezed her again. They all crowded around her in the big family room, crackling with excited energy. "You need a lavish dinner after all that jailhouse food."

"I think I'll make my fortune by writing a book called *The Prison Diet*." She glanced down at her shrunken frame. "I thought I was slender before, but apparently there was plenty of room for improvement if you believe the old saying you can never be too rich or too thin."

"I'm glad your sense of humor survived intact," said RJ. "We Kincaids take some serious lickings."

"Where's Brooke? I heard she came for dinner on Sunday." His mom's sharp green eyes met his.

He hesitated. His mom didn't need to hear any bad news. "She's at home."

"Why don't you invite her to join us?"

RJ glanced at Matt. He knew, as did the others, that Brooke had kept her words with the police secret. Part of him yearned to pick up the phone and invite her back into their lives, but some cooler, more practical instinct told him to maintain distance. "I think it's better if we enjoy your newfound freedom as a family." He didn't comment on the fact that Susannah and Lily and Laurel's fiancés had joined them. He wasn't engaged to Brooke, after all.

"I hope my newfound freedom is permanent. And you all better hope I don't skip out on the two million dollars bail they made you post."

"Cheap at the price, Mom." Matt kissed her slim cheek.

Kara handed Elizabeth a glass of champagne she'd poured. "And if you skip you'd better take us with you. I don't think any of us could stand that kind of separation again."

"Much as I hate everything that's happened to our family in the last few months, there's no denying it's brought us closer than ever." Laurel sat on the sofa next to Eli.

"And now you guys can really start planning your wedding." Kara's eyes lit up. "Mom, Laurel wouldn't even look at invitations until you were released."

"Oh, I think we need some time for things to settle, don't we?" Laurel looked at Eli.

"Sure, yes. A lot going on right now." He patted her hand in a reassuring way. "We have the rest of our lives to plan our wedding."

"Of course you do." Elizabeth Kincaid smiled at the handsome pair. "No sense rushing into marriage. It's a big commitment and sometimes involves a good deal of sacrifice."

RJ could understand Laurel's reluctance to launch into marriage. Especially now they knew their parents' marriage wasn't quite the rosy union they'd grown up imagining.

"Mom." Lily leaned forward. "Did you really know about Dad's second family?"

She hesitated for a moment, then nodded. "Not all the time. Just the last couple of years. I didn't see any reason to burden the rest of you with the news."

"It wasn't right for you to bear it alone." Lily stroked their mom's arm.

"Maybe that's the only way I could bear it." She shrugged her shoulders. "It's a lot harder now the secret's out, and when anyone looks at me I wonder if that's what they're thinking about. Have those two boys been causing any trouble?"

"Jack's stayed out of the picture." RJ frowned at the very thought of Reginald's true oldest son. "So who knows what he's up to. If you ask me he's responsible for the murder. I still can't believe Dad gave him a controlling share of the company." He shook his head and blew out a disgusted breath.

"Alan's been lovely, though," Kara chimed in. "He's really quite sweet. I know he was devastated to hear that you'd been arrested, and he's been very supportive. He seems quite keen to become part of the family, even though he's not related by blood."

"Well, perhaps that's something good to come out of this mess. We Kincaids can always stretch to welcome a new family member." His mom's smile warmed RJ's heart. "And what a relief it is to be back in my own home, surrounded by all of you."

They took champagne glasses from a tray and raised a toast. Still, despite the bubbly and festive mood, a cold sorrow settled in RJ's gut. Brooke should be here. He still resented that she hadn't told him about her talk with the police, but she'd woven herself tightly into the fabric of his life and his arms now felt empty without her in them. He missed her with a painful ache he'd never known before. Was this love? If so it wasn't exactly a happy feeling.

"You okay, RJ?" Laurel nudged him. "You look a bit dazed."

"Overwhelmed, I guess." He took a bracing swig of champagne. "I'll be fine." Already he regretted driving Brooke away in such a cold and cruel manner. Paying her to stay away from him? His shock and anger had gotten the better of him.

And what if she was pregnant? For a single, mad instant, he had a vision of Brooke gazing, with her kind, loving expression, at their baby.

He took another swig. Everything was moving so fast and he didn't know where he'd be from one day to the next. Jack could take over the company and boot him out. The last thing he needed was to establish some kind of permanent relationship. He'd better keep his options open and his feet ready to dodge bullets.

Still, he had to apologize to her.

"Dinner's ready!" Pamela opened the door bearing a steaming dish of food. "Come into the dining room. I set the table already."

The apology would have to wait. He was needed

here for now. RJ followed the others into the elegant dining room, where the silver cloche opened to reveal their mom's favorite roast lamb and potatoes au gratin. Matt poured wine and they settled down to enjoy their first real family dinner since the arrest.

"Okay, let me get this straight." Evie's voice emerged from Brooke's phone, set on speakerphone so she could pace around her living room. "Since I was at your house—oh, two hours ago—and you were telling me you loved RJ, he's now dumped you and fired you."

Brooke inhaled an unsteady breath. She'd already cried once; surely she could keep the tears in for now. "That's pretty much it. I'm not technically fired. I'm on paid leave. In fact he was so keen to get rid of me that he's paying me more to stay home than I'd get to come to the office. He's furious with me."

"All because you neglected to mention that you shopped his mom to the cops."

"Evie! Are you my friend?"

"I'm teasing. You didn't tell him because you thought he'd dump you and fire you. Apparently you were right." She could tell Evie found this slightly funny. "I'm thinking he's not quite so fabulous as you originally told me."

"He's a very passionate, proud family man. He was raised to be head of the Kincaid family, and they come first. I admire that."

"Even when it means you come last?"

Brooke bit her lip hard. "I wish the two weren't mutually exclusive. If I could figure out a way to get his mom out of jail, he might forgive me."

"Elizabeth Kincaid is out of jail!" Evie's voice boomed out of the tiny phone. "I saw it on the news not fifteen minutes ago. She's been granted bail."

"She's out?" RJ hadn't told her. Then again, why would he? He didn't want anything to do with her. Her heart crumpled.

"They showed a video of her leaving the jail. She's one of those people who manages to look like a society matron even in that situation, polite smile at the cameras, and all that."

"That is good news." She shoved a hand through her hair. "RJ must be thrilled. I wonder if they know who the real killer is." If his mom was truly freed, he might not be so angry with her anymore.

"From what you said, it sounds like you and Elizabeth Kincaid were there right at the time the murder was committed. Did you see or hear anything odd?"

"The building was pretty much empty. But apparently the intruder hid somewhere after the murder and crept out when the guard was in the bathroom."

"So they probably snuck in well before the murder. Were there any unfamiliar people around the office?"

"I didn't notice any but it was a very crazy day. There were at least three big meetings, one of them offsite at the architects. I had a terrible time struggling back with all those blueprints." A thought struck her. She stopped pacing and stood still in the center of the room. An entire, fully formed memory sprang into her head. "My God, the blueprints. I brought them to talk with RJ about the plans for the new retail development on the waterfront. RJ went off to a meeting and I came back to the office with armfuls of blueprints. It was right before closing and pouring rain and I ran from the car park to the front door, trying not to get them wet, but I couldn't get into the revolving door."

Suddenly the whole scene was crystal clear in her mind. The fish smell of the rainstorm, her face and hair wet in the heavy shower, big drops splashing on the crucial blueprints.

And a man in a raincoat, who took half of the blueprints, opened the revolving door for her, and stepped in with her.

They'd emerged on the other side and she'd thanked him profusely as he handed back the rest of the tall cylinders of paper, then they'd walked to the bank of elevators. He didn't get in with her, and that was the last she saw of him.

But he hadn't stopped to sign in at the security desk.

"Brooke, have you been struck dumb?"

"The man, who came through the door with me. He was quite tall, but not quite as tall as RJ." Why did her thoughts spring so readily back to him? "He wore one of those felt hats, you know, the Indiana Jones kind."

"I call those jerk hats, because that's the kind of person who usually wears them. In fact my last boyfriend before—"

"Evie! This is important. His hat was dripping from the rain, and he had little round glasses, the kind with the metal rim, thick lenses, so you could barely see his eyes."

"What about his features. Did you recognize him?"

"No. He had a beard and moustache. Damn, I can't remember the color. Gray, maybe? He was an older guy. And he had a Boston accent, I remember it. You know the kind. *I pahked the cahr in Hahrvad Yahd.*"

Evie laughed aloud. "He sounds very suspicious."

"He didn't stand out much at the time. The coat and hat kind of fit, with the rain. It was so wet, and dark, one of those intense, stormy days. Besides, we get quite a few characters at the office, especially since we've branched into real estate. You wouldn't believe the kind of people who just happened to own a derelict dock in North Jersey."

"Or Massachusetts."

"Exactly. I didn't really think anything of it, but since it was five everyone was leaving, security was in the middle of a shift change and he was with me so he breezed by the security desk without anyone stopping him."

"When he wasn't actually with you."

"No. Not at all."

"He could have been waiting for that opportunity."

"I suppose so." A tingle of anticipation—or was it fear—shot up Brooke's spine. "I think this is important."

"You should call RJ and tell him."

For a moment her fingers itched to hang up on Evie and dial RJ immediately. Then an awful thought occurred to her. "Do you think RJ will be happy to hear I let the killer into the building?" If anything, this made things worse.

"Since he's mad at you already, what's the harm?"

Brooke hugged herself, and stared out the window onto the dark street. "I think I should call and tell the police. I can't believe I never thought of this when I first spoke to them. Then again, maybe this guy had a reason to be there? Perhaps he's not relevant at all."

"Or maybe you've just helped to identify Reginald Kincaid's murderer. RJ will be over the moon that you've cleared his mother of all suspicion, and he'll run right over there and ask you to marry him."

Bright moonlight fell at an angle on the cars parked outside, casting long, sharp daggers of light that fell through her window and across her carpet. "I doubt it."

Ten

"Where's Brooke?" Matt appeared in RJ's office doorway, then cast a glance back at Brooke's empty desk.

RJ shoved a hand through his hair. His chest ached and his head hurt. "On a leave of absence." He said it coolly, hoping Matt would drop the subject.

"Is she sick?" His brother looked worried.

"Nope. I just thought it better if she was home for a while. Things were getting too complicated."

Matt cocked his head. "Don't say I didn't warn you."

RJ stood up from his chair and stretched. Or tried to. Every muscle in his body was tight as a bowstring. He felt Brooke's absence like a missing limb. The office seemed dark and empty without her sunny presence. "I didn't plan it. What a cliché, to have an affair with my assistant. I lost my mind."

And then I lost my heart. He cursed the unwanted

thought that sprang into his brain. Another cliché. Mom read him too much poetry when he was a kid.

Matt moved in and closed the door. "Is she making threats?"

"God, no."

"You're angry she didn't tell you she saw Mom on the night of the murder."

"I was angry. I'm still confused by it. And there's something else." Adrenaline pulsed through him. He picked up a paperweight on his desk and studied it in the light. A tiny model ship trapped in glass, sailing nowhere.

Matt raised a brow. "Care to tell me?"

"I forgot to use a condom."

His brother's eyes widened. "You think she's pregnant?"

"No idea yet, but she could be. Can you see how things were getting complicated?" His heart squeezed. Was Brooke sitting somewhere alone and worried? He cursed the violent urge to take her in his arms and comfort her.

"What a mess. Still, it's not nice to banish her when she's worrying about it, too. She didn't mean to get mom into trouble."

"We needed some space. Things were too intense." At least that's how he tried to explain the strange commotion of feelings that left him unsettled and edgy.

"You miss her, don't you?"

RJ placed the paperweight back on the desk with a thud. "I don't know how I feel. Too much happening all at once."

"I know the feeling." Matt grinned. "It all came

thick and fast between me and Susannah. I think you should go with your gut instincts."

"I'm not sure I have any." His gut was in turmoil right now, maybe because he couldn't face breakfast. Or because he couldn't face a day without Brooke in it. "Besides, we have work to do. To make Jack Sinclair richer." He attempted a wry grin.

Matt crossed his arms. "Don't change the subject."

"Why not? Isn't that what we're doing here? You'd think Jack would be here himself pitching in, since he owns forty-five percent of the company. And what's with Nikki stalling on digging into his books?" Phew. He'd managed to get off the topic of Brooke.

Matt shrugged. "I don't think she suspects him of murder as much as you do."

"Me? What about you?"

"I barely know the guy. Too soon to draw any conclusions. Things aren't always what they seem. Besides, I heard from Tony that the police have new eyewitness testimony about a strange man in the building on the day of the murder."

He sat up. "That's great. Details?"

"An older guy in a trilby, with a Boston accent." Matt shrugged. "I can't think of any clients with Boston accents, can you?"

RJ shook his head. "No, but this is great news. I'm going to call Tony for the full scoop. Hopefully they'll drop all charges against Mom and we can put that ugly chapter behind us."

"Brooke is the new eyewitness. Apparently she called the police last night after remembering the man."

RJ froze. Could Brooke have made this new suspect up? For a moment he cursed himself for the disloyal thought. But he didn't trust Brooke anymore. The realization hit him like a fist to the gut.

"Why the grim expression?" Matt shrugged off his jacket and threw it over his arm.

"Seems very convenient that she suddenly remembers a mysterious intruder, right after everyone's angry with her for surreptitiously fingering Mom."

Matt stepped forward and clapped his hand on RJ's upper arm. "Bro, you're all on edge, but Brooke is not the type to lie. That's why she told the police the truth in the first place. We've both worked with her long enough to know it."

Emotion gripped his chest like a nutcracker. He knew Matt was right. "She never did lie, she just didn't tell me the whole truth." He rubbed his forehead. "Because she was afraid the truth would upset me. If anything, it's my fault she kept silent." He blew out a hard breath. "I owe her an apology." His neurons fired with energy, spurring him forward. "I'm going over to her house."

Matt grinned. "Glad to hear it. I hope she'll forgive you for overreacting."

RJ grabbed his jacket off the back of the chair and pulled it on. "Me, too."

Brooke didn't know what to do. It was midmorning and usually she'd have sorted through a ream of mail and coordinated several schedules and possibly attended a meeting or two. This morning all she'd done was drink a cup of coffee (decaf in case she was pregnant), do some halfhearted yoga poses and dust her bookshelves. She'd be wise to start looking for another job, but she didn't have the heart.

She let out a long sigh and poured the dregs of her coffee into the kitchen sink. She felt like someone had taken a hunting knife to her chest and cut her heart right out of it. All the excitement and happiness of yesterday had crashed and burned so fast she was still too numb to even react properly. She knew pain was coming but right now she was still too shocked and dazed for it to touch her.

How quickly RJ had gone from cherishing her to despising her. He must have never really cared about her in the first place. A sharp pang of disappointment stung her. She still cared about him. She should be angry with him for dismissing her so harshly, but she couldn't blame him. He was under stress and his family came first. She knew both those things before they got involved.

It was her own stupid fault she wasn't brave enough to tell the truth about seeing his mom there that evening and telling the police. Now he'd learn that she let the killer into the building, which was hardly likely to help him forgive her.

She brought her empty coffee cup down on the sideboard with a light thunk. What a mess. Still, time to get dressed. No sense spending the day moping around in her pajamas. If she was pregnant she'd need to be strong for her child, and she might as well start now, just in case.

She'd turned on the shower and started to take off her PJs when the doorbell rang. She frowned. The mail had already been delivered and no one could expect her home at this time. She pulled her T-shirt back down again, turned off the water. Maybe it was the police. She'd spoken to a detective at the station yesterday and they said they might want to speak to her again. She grabbed a robe off the back of the door and slid her arms into it. She couldn't face those flint-eyed officers in her heart-print shorts and top.

As she slid back the chain and undid the lock she couldn't stop a massive, painful flash of hope that it might be RJ on the other side. This in no way diminished her surprise when she opened the door to his tall, imposing presence on her doorstep, dressed in a dark suit.

"May I come in?" His deep voice barely penetrated her shock. She hadn't said a word.

Her pulse now pounded hard and fast. "Yes." She stepped aside and he walked in. Didn't try to kiss her. Didn't shake hands. Still, a rush of energy crashed through her as his body passed within inches of hers.

She closed the door behind him and turned to face him, still no idea what to say. Why was he here?

His bold blue eyes met hers. "I've missed you."

"I've missed you, too." The words fell from her mouth. So much for playing it cool. "Very much." She bit her lip to stop more confessions pouring forth.

"I've come to apologize." His eyes darkened. Brooke held her breath. "Banishing you from the office was out of line. I've been on edge, upset about my mom being in jail. I overreacted to hearing that you were the eyewitness." Morning light shone through the window onto his hard profile.

"I should have told you it was me. I kept trying to pluck up the courage to tell you, but I was so afraid you'd be angry, and I only made it worse."

His expression softened. "My behavior proved you were right. I flew off the handle and it was inappropriate." He hesitated. The air thickened with tension and anticipation until Brooke felt faint. "I'm sorry."

Sorry. Her heart sank. What had she hoped for? He was sorry. For sending her home. For sleeping with her without a condom. For sleeping with her at all. For kissing her. For ever hiring her in the first place…

Her head hurt and she fought to keep herself from shaking, as RJ's tall presence filled her living room.

"Brooke." He stepped forward, and again, pathetic hope rushed through her like a burst water main. He took her hands. Her fingers tingled and heated inside his. "All these years we worked together, sitting in meetings and discussing correspondence and spending all day with each other." She held herself steady. "And all along I never realized I was working side by side with the perfect woman for me."

She blinked. The perfect woman for him? Her tongue seemed stuck in her mouth. Surely she should say something here, but no words rose from her confused and anxious brain.

"I love you, Brooke." His voice deepened as he said the words, and something dark and powerful flashed in his eyes. "I've felt empty and hollow every second I've been without you. All I could think about is coming to see you, to hold you in my arms, and beg you to forgive my cruel behavior. When I thought I might have made you pregnant I panicked about making our lives more complicated than they already are."

He hesitated, frowned slightly, and looked away. Brooke's stomach turned over. Doubts crept back into her mind. Maybe he was just here trying to "do the right thing" in case she was pregnant. Her hands grew cold inside the cocoon of his fingers.

"Brooke, I want to marry you." His eyes met hers again, with a jolt. "I want to have children with you. I want to spend the rest of my life with you." His words, spoken fast and gruff, wrapped around her and swirled through her mind. Did she imagine them? Was this some kind of crazy dream or delusion? It couldn't possibly be happening, right here in her living room, on an ordinary weekday morning.

Could it?

"Brooke, are you okay?"

"I...I don't know." She searched his face. His strong features were taut with emotion. "What did you say?" Her ears must be deceiving her.

One of his dimples appeared. "I said I want to marry you." His eyes twinkled. "You, Brooke Nichols, and me, RJ Kincaid, getting married."

She drew in a ragged breath. He wanted to marry her? Her heart soared, then her excitement screeched to a halt again. Better clear the air. "Is this because I might be pregnant?"

"Not in the least. I want to live the rest of my life with you, for better or for worse. For richer for poorer. All that stuff. How does that sound?"

"It sounds...good." Joy sparkled over her. What an insane roller coaster her life had been lately. Suddenly she'd shot up the ladder to the top of the game board again, and could hear party whistles and see streamers as she approached the final square. Images of her and RJ, walking down a church aisle hand in hand, flooded her mind. "Really good."

Then something hit her like an icy thunderbolt.

RJ didn't know that she had likely let his father's

killer into the building. That she was, in some way, responsible for his dad's death.

Her joy drained away.

"What's the matter? You've turned pale." RJ's dimples disappeared again.

"You don't know, do you?"

"Know what?"

She swallowed. Her hands tightened into cold fists inside his grasp. "I let the killer into the building."

RJ dropped her hands as if they burned. "What are you talking about?"

Pain trickled through her as his expression darkened. She inhaled a shaky breath. "I remembered, when I thought hard, that a strange man came through the revolving doors with me. I didn't think anything of it at the time, since I didn't know him. There's no record of him and no one knows who he is. In all likelihood he went to hide somewhere, and then…" She gulped. "Shot your dad later that night."

She looked down at the floor, not wanting to see RJ's appalled expression.

"Matt told me you'd seen someone and that you spoke to the police again." His voice was strangely hollow. "He didn't say you opened the door for him."

"He was just another person hurrying into the building on a stormy afternoon. It was right at the end of the day. I didn't really even register him at the time." Tears rose inside her. "I'm so, so sorry." She looked up, to find RJ's eyes filled with pain.

But instead of striding away, he stepped toward her and took her in his arms. "I know you'd never do anything to hurt my family, or the company." His warmth enveloped her, and the stirring male scent of him soothed her ragged nerves. "We all know that." He pulled away from her long enough to look her in the eye. "No one blames you for Dad's death. The good part is now we have a real suspect and the police can go after him." She shuddered as he buried his face in her neck and his breath heated her skin. "And I can't even tell you how much I've missed you." His words swirled around her, spoken with gruff passion.

"I've missed you, too." Her voice sounded so small. Her heart filled so fast with all the hope and love she'd locked away in the last day, thinking she'd never need it again. He'd told her he loved her! "I love you, RJ. A part of me has loved you for years, but since we became close..." Words failed her, which didn't matter because RJ's mouth covered hers in a heady kiss.

He pulled her tight against his muscled chest and she sank into his strength. When their lips parted, she felt his chest fill with a mighty breath. "God, Brooke, I couldn't stand my life without you in it. Can you ever forgive me for being such a jerk?"

His wry expression almost made her laugh. "You were under stress. You're still under stress."

"We all are, but that's no excuse for the way I behaved. I'll do anything in my power to make it up to you." His face hovered close to hers, kissing and nuzzling her, stirring sparks of arousal that mingled with her joy to create an electric atmosphere.

"I don't want anything from you." She stroked his hair, and relished the rough feel of his hard cheek against hers. "I just want you."

RJ's ragged breath revealed the depth of his emotion. "And I just want you. Will you, Brooke? Will you marry me?"

"Yes." The tiny voice emerged from somewhere deep inside her. Somewhere hope had survived during all the drama and upset of the last few weeks. "I will."

They held each other tight, half-afraid some fresh drama would fly in through the window to blow them apart again. They stayed silent for some time, then RJ spoke. "It's okay if you're pregnant. In fact, it's more than okay." He pulled back far enough to meet her eyes. "Once again I overreacted and lost sight of the big picture. I'd love to have a child with you, Brooke."

Her chest tightened, or was it her heart that swelled even further? "Me, too." She smiled. "Though there's an excellent chance that I'm not pregnant, so don't get too excited. I wasn't at the right place in my cycle."

"Then we'll just have to try again." Hope sparkled in his eyes. "Because I see us having a big family."

Brooke swallowed. She'd always dreamed of a house filled with children, so unlike her solitary childhood. "I'd love to have a big family, like yours."

"Then we'll need a big house. Maybe a historic one near downtown? Or would you prefer something out in the suburbs?"

"I love downtown. It's nice to be able to walk to the shops, and restaurants. And work." She froze. Work. Would they keep working together after they were married, or would that be too weird?

RJ raised a brow. "Are you thinking what I'm thinking?"

"I'm not quite telepathic enough to know. But I was wondering if I'm still banished from the office."

"Definitely not. But I think you should move into your own office. You've done enough time manning the desk outside mine. I think it's time you're promoted to management."

Brooke blinked. So he had remembered their conversation where she'd shared her career goals? The subject hadn't come up again so she'd tried to forget about it. "I'd love that. I'm happy to work at The Kincaid Group in any capacity, but I'd like to stretch myself and develop new skills that can help the company."

RJ laughed. "Hey, you're not on a job interview. I already know you're an organizational genius. And if things go south with Jack Sinclair running the show, maybe we can start our own company together."

She smiled. "That might be fun."

"I think anything we do together will be fun, as long as we can keep our perspective, and I promise I've learned a lot about myself over the last day or so." He took a deep breath. "From now on I'll put our relationship first and everything else second. Or even third." His dimples appeared. "Or fourth."

A sudden thought clouded Brooke's happiness. "What will your mom think about us?"

"She'll be thrilled." He stroked her cheek. "I couldn't understand why no one, including her, would tell me who the eyewitness was. Later I realized she didn't want me to know it was you. She really likes you. She asked about you several times during dinner last night."

"She doesn't mind that I'm not from local aristocracy?" She couldn't help voicing the worry that had nagged at her from the first time RJ asked her out.

"Not at all. Mom judges people on their own merits, not the arcane rules of the society she was born into.

That's why she married my dad, even though a lot of the local snobs thought him beneath her."

"I don't think I'll ever understand the rules of Charleston society."

"Don't waste time trying, because they don't make any sense." He kissed her on the nose, which brought a smile to her lips. "We'll make our own rules to live by."

Their mouths met in a kiss that melted the tension in her body and replaced it with a flush of pleasure. RJ's arms enclosed her in their protective circle. Everything they'd been through hadn't torn them apart forever, but had pulled them closer together.

"Rule number one," she breathed, when they finally parted lips for a few moments. "No shoving me off on paid leave when I get on your nerves."

RJ winced. "I made a real ass of myself. If you can't ever forgive me for that, I can understand."

"I'll let you off just this one time." She dotted a kiss on the end of his nose. "Since you're devastatingly handsome." The sheepish look in his slate blue eyes made her smile.

"That's quite a compliment coming from the loveliest woman in Charleston."

"Flatterer."

"It's all true. Best figure, too." He squeezed her rear. "And since I seem to have talked my way back from the brink of disaster, I hope I'll be sharing a bed with it tonight." He grew still and his gaze darkened. "You did say you'd marry me, didn't you?"

Brooke chewed her lip and pretended to look confused. "Did I?"

"I think you did but it might have been wishful thinking."

She shrugged her shoulders. Arousal trickled through her like hot liquid. "It's been a confusing time, lately. Maybe we should stop talking and just go to bed right now."

RJ's dimples appeared. "That's the best idea I've heard in a long time."

* * * * *

Turn the page for an exclusive short story
by USA TODAY bestselling author Day Leclaire.
Then look for the next installment of
DYNASTIES: THE KINCAIDS,
ON THE VERGE OF I DO,
by Heidi Betts
wherever Harlequin books are sold.

THE KINCAIDS: JACK AND NIKKI, PART 3

Day Leclaire

Morning came, streaks of blushing red, glittering amber and a deep bruising purple. It gave an incredible punctuation mark to what had been another amazing night and offered a joyous wakeup kiss to what Nikki Thomas hoped would be an equally amazing day.

She stood on the deck of Jack Sinclair's beach house, a place she'd frequently stood since that morning after they'd first made love. Of course, the term "beach house" seemed such a ridiculous description for such an elegant, stylish home. Beach mansion came closer to describing it. She rested her forearms on the salt-treated wooden railing and stared out at the ball of fire heaving itself from greenish-blue water. Breakers curled in long, uniform sets, rolling toward shore, and she drew in a deep breath of fragrant, salt-laden air, filled with the wealth of springtime promise.

Had she ever experienced anything more idyllic? A

pair of strong, masculine arms slid around her, pulling her against a broad, naked chest, as powerful and indomitable as the ocean stretching toward the horizon. She released a sigh and relaxed against Jack. Okay, *this* was more idyllic.

"Is that coffee I smell?" she asked.

"Maybe. How grateful would you be if I brought you a cup?"

"Very grateful." She turned, wrapped her arms around his neck and drew him down for a deep, lingering kiss. Dear Lord, the man could kiss, his lips firm and possessive and slightly crafty, edging a simple caress into something that had her melting against him in desperate longing. "In fact, I might be grateful enough to make us both late for work."

"Tempting. More than tempting." Regret shimmered in his eyes, the early morning sunlight catching in the robin's egg blue intensity of them. "Unfortunately, I have a meeting at The Kincaid Group today."

"With your...your father's family?" As if she didn't know.

"The Legitimates," he confirmed. "The legitimate side of the family tree, forced to deal with the bastard in the family. My father's dirty little secret."

Where before his expression had been open and relaxed, now it hardened, reminding Nikki that the man with whom she'd been having a passionate affair for the past month was considered one of the most ruthless businessmen in all of Charleston, South Carolina. She'd do well to remember that. Not that a single day or night went by without her worrying about his unearthing the secret she continued to keep from him....

How would he react if he ever discovered she worked for The Kincaid Group? That as their corporate investigator, she'd been assigned to investigate *him*. To dig into his corporate activities in order to determine whether he'd been working on the sly to damage TKG as part of an effort to absorb the company into his own, Carolina Shipping.

Of course, her affair with him had begun weeks before RJ Kincaid assigned her to the investigation. But that didn't change a thing. Eventually the truth would come out about her role at TKG and their affair would end. Badly. Equally as bad, she doubted the Kincaids would take it well if they found out she and Jack were involved in an intimate relationship.

But until that happened, she intended to treasure every single minute. Indulge herself to the fullest. And hope, desperately, that a solution presented itself, one that would take her out of the equation. Not likely to happen, particularly considering she had another secret, one she'd kept from Jack *and* the Kincaids. A secret that kept her squarely between all the various combatants in this little war.

"What about you?" he asked. "Still working on your top secret project for your top secret employer?"

It was the story she'd given him when their involvement blossomed into something more serious than the dinner date with him she'd won through a charity auction. He'd asked about her job when they'd first become involved and because she'd been unwilling to face a fast end to an amazing relationship, she'd told him the information was confidential. Well, it hadn't been a total lie. What she did for TKG was most definitely confidential, even if the identity of her employers wasn't. Fortunately, due to the nature of her work the Kincaids kept her name very low-key, on a need-to-know basis only.

She rested her head against his shoulder so she wouldn't have to look at him, so he wouldn't see the guilt that must be written all over her face. "Yes, still working on that project."

He captured her chin in his hand and tilted it upward. "Just reassure me about one thing," he insisted. "Promise me you aren't in any danger."

Oh, God. How did she answer that? Yes, she was in danger. In terrible danger. In danger of losing her heart to a man she could never have, a man she wanted more than any she'd ever known, but who could never share a future with her.

"I'm in no physical danger," she informed him.

"Swear it."

"I swear it." She risked a quick, teasing smile. "Now do I get coffee?"

"I think I can make that happen."

He drew her up for another kiss, one as hot and potent as the sun at her back, filling her with warmth and a sweet, sharp desire. How was it possible that she'd tumbled so fast? That in just one short month Jack could come to mean so much to her? It was frightening and wonderful and ultimately tragic when their relationship couldn't end any other way than badly. Even with the knowledge ripping through her, she wrapped her arms around his neck and surrendered to a bottomless passion.

With a groan of demand, Jack swept her into his arms and carried her through the French doors leading from the deck to his bedroom. She dropped her head to his shoulder and snuggled into the embrace. "Bringing me to the coffee instead of the coffee to me?" she asked.

"Not quite."

Nikki's breath hitched as she recognized the intent beneath the clipped words. "What about your meeting with the Kincaids?"

"Some things are more important." He lowered her to the bed, followed her down. The fit of angles to curves caused her to shudder from the intensity of her need, from the helplessness of it. "Right now, you're the most important thing in my world."

She closed her eyes. "Please don't say that."

He brushed her hair back from her face, tracing the line of her jaw and cheekbones. Lingering in a scintillating caress. "Why not?"

She looked at him then, saw something in his eyes, something she didn't want to identify. Something she suspected was reflected in her own. "Because it's perfect," she whispered helplessly.

A smile eased the hard, tough curve of his mouth, turning his customary ruthlessness into something that made him approachable. Something and someone she could lose herself in, who put her heart at serious risk. "Maybe there's a reason for that," he replied, his eyes dark and serious.

Not a reason she dared look at. Not now. "Why you?" she demanded. "Why did it have to be you?"

"I don't have a clue."

She pulled him down, inhaled him, drew him in. "Maybe because I'm a lucky, lucky woman."

He smiled with a tenderness that devastated. "You have that backward, sweetheart. I'm the lucky one."

* * *

After escaping Jack's bed, Nikki decided to work from home that morning in order to avoid running into him at TKG. She emailed RJ Kincaid to warn him that she wouldn't be in until after lunch. He shot her back an immediate response asking her to join him at her earliest convenience, no doubt so they could discuss his meeting with Jack.

She arrived at the office to find the three Kincaids most intimately involved in the daily running of The Kincaid Group just concluding a meeting in the main conference room. Matthew Kincaid, tall and sporting a swimmer's physique, lounged back in one of the leather swivel chairs, a look of concern disturbing the even tenor of his expression while he listened to his sister.

"This could turn into a nightmare from a PR standpoint," Laurel Kincaid was saying. As tall as Nikki, the eldest Kincaid daughter was a stunning redhead, the image of her mother. "We can't allow Sinclair to throw any question on the stability of TKG by claiming he's going to run the company once we elect our new CEO at the June meeting."

"And gaining new business between now and then will also be problematic," Matthew added. "Who wants to hire a company who may not have a Kincaid at the helm in another three months?"

RJ nodded wearily. "We've been around this and around it and I don't see an easy solution. We have got to find something to hang Sinclair with. Speaking of which..." He waved Nikki into the room. "We'd appreciate an update. Please tell us you've found something. Anything."

Oh, God. What did she say? Nikki cleared her throat

and wished with every fiber of her being that RJ didn't look so much like Jack. But the two were definitely their father's sons. Tough features, deeply scored by sophistication and experience, they both had a multitude of life's lessons marking the striking blue brilliance of their eyes. Each was also tall and broad, their muscular builds delineated by the superb cut of their suits. Even the deep tenor of their voices was uncannily similar, which had caught her off guard more than once over the past two months.

"So far everything checks out," she said. "I wish for all your sakes, that it didn't. Carolina Shipping is a solid company with a sterling reputation. There have only been two lawsuits against Jack Sinclair. I'd classify them as nuisance suits, both settled in his favor."

"What about on the personal front?" Matthew's green eyes sharpened on her. "You've socialized with him, right?"

RJ looked momentarily startled by the question before making the connection and nodding. "Of course. The bachelor auction. Your dinner date." He edged his hip onto the conference table and folded his arms across his chest. "The family has only associated with him at the lawyer's office and in a business setting. His half brother, Alan, has surprised me by being downright friendly. Seems a decent enough sort. As for Sinclair… I couldn't get a true personal read on the SOB. He's much more self-contained."

Laurel sighed. "Our meetings with Jack couldn't be considered the best circumstances in which to get to know anyone, let alone our—surprise—half brother."

RJ's mouth tightened. "Assuming we wanted to get to know him." At the mention of Jack's name, his eyes took on an expression identical to Jack's whenever the Kincaid name was mentioned. It was downright freaky, not to mention distressing. "Which we don't. Maybe if he was as innocuous as Alan, it might have been a different story. But it's clear he despises us. And equally clear he'd like to destroy TKG."

"He doesn't realize you work for us, does he, Nikki?" Matthew asked in concern.

She shook her head. "No. I've kept that quiet."

"Give us your assessment of him on a personal level," RJ prompted.

Nikki hesitated, choosing her words with care. "He's more relaxed. I guess he would be all things considered. Still hard. Still tough. But if I were to attempt to describe him, I'd say…" Her gaze arrowed toward RJ and she shrugged. "He's a lot like you."

Insult spread across his face, spiked through his body and he straightened. "That's a hell of a thing to say."

She refused to back down from her assessment. "You know I call it like I see it. You're both a lot like your father. You have boundaries and God help anyone who steps across those lines. You're both brilliant businessmen. But when crossed you're…" She forced herself to acknowledge the truth. "Ruthless."

RJ took a moment to absorb her words before nodding. "No doubt Brooke would agree with that description."

Matthew continued to watch Nikki with a sharpness she tried to ignore. He opened his mouth to speak, then much to her relief, reconsidered. "We need more information than you have so far. Insider information. Information that will help us by June."

Now it was Laurel watching her, this time with a woman's gaze and a woman's understanding. "Are we done here, guys?"

The two men nodded. After thanking Nikki, they switched to a shorthand wrap-up on a business matter on the way out the door. Laurel lingered, touching Nikki's arms with unmistakable sympathy. "Would you rather we assign someone else to research Sinclair?" she asked gently. "I can arrange it without raising any flags with my brothers."

The offer tempted Nikki beyond measure. Even so, she shook her head. "I can do my job."

"Is it serious?"

A smile wobbled across her mouth. "It won't be when he finds out I work for TKG." Normally, she wouldn't have been so forthcoming, especially since she was concerned about how her affair with Jack would affect her job. But something about Laurel's calm, understanding gaze had her opening up. "Of course, if he somehow manages to gain control of the company, working for him won't be a problem since I'm sure his first act will be to fire me."

Laurel's laughter held a dry edge. "Right after he fires us." Her green eyes turned defiant. "Not that that's going to happen. Not while we have anything to say about it."

"I wouldn't do anything to betray your family," Nikki stated, aware it needed to be said. "You know that, don't you?"

Laurel nodded without a moment's hesitation. "We all know it. My father once told me you took after your father. That one of the defining qualities you shared was an unswerving sense of honor. It's part of what made him such an outstanding policeman and has made you such a valuable employee."

The observation caused tears to prick Nikki's eyes. "Thank you for telling me that about my father. It means the world to me that others saw him the way I did. As for me…" She closed her eyes. "Somehow I'm not feeling too honorable about the way I've handled all this."

And she didn't. She'd kept a secret from both parties, a secret she'd promised Reginald Kincaid she'd keep. But in order to honor that promise, it compromised what she considered her integrity and duty on another front. And then there was the lie she lived with Jack. She should have been up-front with him about who she worked for right from the beginning. She'd planned to tell him over that first dinner together after she'd placed the winning bid at the bachelor's auction. Instead of alerting him to the connection, she'd slept with him. Granted, the next morning she had intended to confess the truth. Would have if he hadn't said one small thing that had stilled her tongue….

It was the morning after their bachelor auction dinner date. The morning following the first night they'd made love. Nikki woke to find Jack standing on the deck just off his bedroom, brought him a cup of coffee and a confession. But one look at the brooding starkness on his face made her hesitate a moment too long.

He held a thick envelope in his hands that reeked money and class, and tapped it against the railing as though the contents contained a terrible emotional burden. It was heavily creased and careworn, but still sealed. She caught The Kincaid Group's distinctive logo decorating one corner, the ink blurred from frequent handling. "I'm taking them down, you know," he announced.

Even though she guessed who he meant, she forced herself to ask. "Who are you taking down, Jack?"

"The Kincaids." He turned, accepted the coffee with a hard smile, remained blissfully unaware her confession had slipped away like a forgotten dream. "Ironic, isn't it? By giving me 45 percent interest in TKG, my own father handed me the very weapon I needed to destroy his family. Why do you suppose he'd do that?"

"Maybe he didn't consider it a weapon," she suggested hesitantly. "Maybe he hoped you'd realize they're your family, too."

"They're not my family," he instantly retorted. "They will *never* be my family."

Nikki waited a beat so he'd hear the anger and defensiveness in his own voice before deliberately instilling a hint of calm in her reply. "Then maybe your father considered it an olive branch, an attempt to correct past errors in judgment."

Jack drew a deep breath and gathered himself. "Could be. There's one way I could find out." Steam from the mug caused a curtain to form between them while he sipped, before parting again when he set the mug on top of the envelope, pinning it to the railing. "I can tell that startles you."

"Only because your father's dead, so I'm not sure how you can get any real answers."

He flicked a corner of the envelope. "He left me a personal note. And no doubt a lengthy explanation for why he refused to acknowledge me all these years.

Why he never told the Legitimates that I existed. Why he felt it acceptable to betray his wife and take my mother for his mistress. I wonder if he asks for forgiveness or simply attempts to excuse his behavior."

She glanced again at the seal. "You haven't opened it. Why?"

"Because I'm tempted to burn it."

"Unread?"

He turned to her, genuine amusement brightening the intense blue of his gaze. "You think I'd regret it if I destroyed the damn thing without reading it?"

"I..." She almost said, "I don't know." But she did know. There wasn't a single doubt in her mind. "Yes. Yes, I think you'd regret it. If not now, at some point."

He turned back to the letter, lifted the mug for another swallow of coffee. A bitter-dark ring marred the creamy white of the envelope. A dark smudge that reflected Jack's birthright...or birth wrong. And yet, a ring that connected all the Kincaids within that unfortunate darkness. "I decided to give it more time for just that reason. First impulses aren't always the best choice."

"Bidding for you at the auction was a first impulse. So was sleeping with you."

He leaned in, soothed the worry from her brow with a tender kiss. "The exception that proves the rule."

Confession time. "Listen, Jack, there's something you should know—"

"There are some who suspect—hope—I killed my father."

Damn, damn, damn. "Did you kill Reginald Kincaid?" she asked evenly.

She asked the question deliberately, hoping to jar

Jack out of his odd mood. And that's when she saw it. The stillness. The flash of pain. The weary acceptance. Each expression reflected an emotion she knew—knew without a minute's doubt—he'd experienced countless times in the past, a lifetime's accumulation of slights and insults he'd absorbed, all of which had left scars. How many were due to his birth? How many to the fact that he was Reginald Kincaid's son by blood, but never by name? How many were because his mother was Kincaid's mistress? How many were because he'd lived his entire life in the shadows, unable to claim kith or kin, always living beneath a cloud of shame?

She went to him, took the coffee from his hand and set it aside. She wrapped him up in the warmth of her embrace, waiting for his instinctive resistance to fade. Little by little he surrendered to the comfort she offered. The instant he rested his cheek against the top of her head she knew she'd won him over, eased some tiny part of his burden.

She also knew she couldn't tell him about her ties to the Kincaids, that to do so would cut him adrift once again. She couldn't do that to him. Even more, she couldn't do it to herself. She wasn't ready to lose him. If she toed the line she always had in the past, the line that demanded she follow a certain code of honor, he would end things between them before they fully began. And she wasn't ready for that.

Nikki cupped the back of Jack's head and lifted her face to his, drawing him down and into a slow, lush kiss. Warmth flooded over them, capturing them within the brilliant rays of the sun, adding even more heat to their embrace. He ran his hands over the simple silk shirt she wore—his shirt from the night before.

And then he swept under, tracing the naked curves he found beneath. It made her desperately grateful he owned extensive land around his home and had planted trees that blocked any possibility of being seen, other than from the empty stretch of beach.

He cupped her buttocks, lifting her against the rigid line of his arousal, aligning her more acutely to sheer masculinity. Then upward still further to cup the fullness of her breasts. His thumbs traced the tight peaks of her nipples and he inhaled her groan of pleasure, incorporated it into their kiss.

"I want you." He backed her toward one of the large, cushioned deck loungers and came down on top of her. "I can't seem to stop wanting you."

"Make love to me. Here and now."

"Not my usual venue."

She laughed, filled with a recklessness she'd never experienced before other than with him. Only with him. "I have a confession."

"You're secretly a Kincaid?" he teased. She stiffened, unable to help herself, her shock communicating itself to him. His eyes narrowed in abrupt suspicion. "Tell me you're not somehow related to the Kincaids and are secretly on their side in our little war."

"I'm not secretly related to the Kincaids," she answered without hesitation, the truth of her modified statement reflected in her eyes and voice.

"Swear it."

"I swear it."

"Sorry." He shook his head and released a gruff laugh. "These days I'm seeing Kincaids lurking behind every tree. Maybe because half the time they are."

She ran her hands over his chest, hoping to distract

him, tracing the ridges of power that rippled across the impressive expanse. It worked like a charm. He shuddered beneath the gentle caress. One by one he opened the buttons of her shirt—his shirt—and spread the silk wide. She lay beneath him, utterly exposed, so bared she worried that he could see straight through to her heart and soul and those tiny secrets that hid there. He cupped her breast, lowered his head to nip, to pleasure. She surrendered to him, helpless to do anything less. All he had to do was touch her and she was his for the taking.

He took his time, exploring where the sun dappled. Somehow making them one with the give and take of the sea. The pounding surf that echoed the kick of her heart. The swish of water dragging across sand that matched the movement of his mouth and tongue across her body. The desperate, helpless drive of salt water against shoreline that mirrored the desperate, helpless drive of passion that sent her climbing, climbing, climbing. The relentless rush that couldn't be stopped before the break of wave, the powerful tumble that nature demanded.

Her cry of climax joined with that of the sea, with that of the man whose body mated with hers. And in that moment she realized there was no going back. Not now. Not ever. No matter how this ended. Slowly they subsided, the crash easing to bliss. They held and clung for untracked time.

He turned his head to meet her stunned gaze. "Still think I killed my father?" he asked.

She winced, aware she'd hit a serious hot button earlier. She rolled onto her side and snuggled in. "Considering you just sent me straight to heaven, I may have to rethink my original opinion."

He chuckled, tucking her closer still. "You asked me that question deliberately, didn't you? Not because that's what you believe, but rather to watch my reaction. Did you learn that technique from your father?"

"Guilty," she confessed, her voice muffled against his shoulder.

"Quite effective. I'll have to try it sometime, maybe with the Kincaids."

"Oh, Jack." She tilted her head back and looked up at him. "How will ruining the Kincaids solve anything? It won't make Reginald any more or less your father. It won't change how you were raised."

"Let's just say I'll find it satisfying."

"To ruin The Kincaid Group?"

He lifted a dark eyebrow. "Who said anything about ruining the company? That would be counterproductive, since I now own 45 percent."

She relaxed ever so slightly. Maybe she'd misread the situation. "Oh. Well, okay then."

"No, I want TKG to prosper when I take it over and one by one take each and every last Kincaid down. They've had their reign. They've spent their entire lives at the top. Reginald Kincaid's sons and daughters. The Legitimates." Ruthless intent burned in Jack's eyes, carved a pathway across his features. "Now it's my turn. Now the Kincaid bastard takes over."

And that's when Nikki realized she was in serious trouble, that she'd put herself in an impossible situation, one in which she felt honor-bound to protect both sides in a war no one could possibly win. The only thing she knew with dead certainty…

When this war ended, she would be the ultimate loser.

* * * * *

THE ROYAL COUSIN'S REVENGE

Catherine Mann

One

Javier Cortez walked onto the private jet as coolly as he'd walked out of Victoria Palmer's life a year ago.

Seeing him, Victoria gripped the armrests, her short fingernails digging into the butter-soft leather. If only there were other passengers inside the luxury craft. If only the pilot wasn't behind a closed door to the cockpit.

If only she'd had some warning Javier would be on this flight, too.

But he'd caught her unawares and unprepared. And without question, she needed all her defenses in place around this man.

He noticed her then and his eyes locked on hers, his expression as enigmatic and unreadable as always. Javier rarely showed emotion.

Except when he'd made love to her.

Her eyes tracked her former lover as he strode toward her.

What was he doing on this flight? Why was he even in Boston instead of at home in Martha's Vineyard?

She'd contracted to be a private nurse for his uncle on his family's private island off the Florida coast—the post she'd had when she'd met Javier more than a year ago. She'd agreed to work for his uncle for only a week this time, balking at stepping back into this family's world. But the old man had offered her quite a sum...and she couldn't afford to say no. She needed the money to pay her brother's lawyer.

Javier shifted his briefcase from one hand to the other, tucking the monogrammed case beside a seat. Defined muscles rippled under his wool suit—vicuña. She still remembered the feel of the exclusive texture in her hands as she tore the clothes from his body.

She couldn't seem to stop looking at him. His coal-black hair was swept back from his broad forehead. The sharp angles of his face spoke of his aristocratic heritage. Javier Cortez had—no kidding—royal Medina blood coursing through his veins. His uncle had ruled a small island country off the coast of Spain until a violent coup more than twenty-five years ago.

The Medinas and their Cortez relatives had lived in anonymity until recently when the press had caught wind of their royal roots.

Not that she'd cared a bit about his blue blood—not then, and not now. She'd cared about the man. The recent media exposé on his family had etched stress lines in the corners of Javier's eyes. Not that he would ever admit to any vulnerability.

His family may have relocated to America, but his

regal Castilian heritage couldn't be denied. And his raw magnetism couldn't be missed.

A shiver of awareness, of desire, skittered up her spine. How would she maintain the necessary distance from him until they reached Florida?

Her mouth went dry as he stopped beside her seat. The spicy scent of his bay rum soap drifted along the recycled air.

"Why are you here?" he demanded.

"You remember me?" She couldn't resist the jab, given how unemotionally he'd walked toward her.

"Don't be ridiculous." He waved aside the barb with an autocratic flick of his hand. "And don't be coy. Why are you here?"

Irritation simmered.

"I live in Boston. If anything, I should be asking you the question."

"This is a Medina plane, and you, Victoria Palmer, are not a Medina."

"But I am, once again, on the Medina payroll. Your uncle hired me to help with his nursing care. With his sons visiting, he wants to make the most of his time with them."

Enrique Medina was slowly dying of liver failure caused by injuries he'd suffered while on the run from the rebels who'd ousted him from his homeland of San Rinaldo. The deposed king still lived in isolation on an island off the coast of Florida, where she'd cared for him the first time. Where she and Javier had begun their affair.

A Medina cousin, Javier worked for Enrique's son on Martha's Vineyard as head of security for their resort. A year ago, he had been visiting his uncle's mansion to check on the island's safety.

One look at the brooding Javier and Victoria had fallen for him. She'd changed jobs to relocate and live near him. Their affair had lasted four months. But she'd let sexual attraction blind her to how wrong they were for each other. How very unbending and arrogant the man could be.

He'd broken her heart. He'd wrecked her family.

She wouldn't be a fool for him again.

"You should sit so we can take off," she said coolly.

Victoria pulled her romance novel from beside her in the seat, hoping he would get the message and leave her alone.

The scent of his soap intoxicated her all the more as he slid onto the sofa across from her, his knees almost brushing hers.

He snapped his seat belt on smoothly, without once looking away from her. "Why wasn't I told of your arrival?"

A dry smile tugged at her lips. "Maybe your uncle didn't want to listen to you gripe about having me around."

A lone eyebrow rose arrogantly. "He asked me to make upgrades to his security. That means I have to know everyone who comes and goes from the island. Anything I may or may not feel is of no significance."

Sheesh. Now, didn't that just put her in her place? Anger knocked against her ribs. Anger, not attraction, particularly since he'd just made it clear he didn't care about her either way.

"Well, now you know. I'm going to the island." She put on her headphones and opened her novel.

And nearly groaned as she realized her bookmarked place stopped right at a particularly steamy love scene.

Javier Cortez hated surprises. He'd experienced firsthand the high price of being caught unawares and unprepared, ousted from his homeland as a kid, chased by rebels who'd killed his grandparents and his aunt. Settling deeper into his seat as the private plane soared upward, he studied his ex-lover reading her novel—or pretending to read, since her page-turning was suspiciously random. He was a man who liked to be in control, and Victoria Palmer was one huge jolt to his system. She dulled his instincts and rattled his focus. She was also still hot as hell. He wouldn't be able to stand up anytime soon without revealing just how much she still affected him. Her blond hair was gathered in a sleek ponytail that trailed over one shoulder. He ached to ease that simple cloth band down the length of her hair and free the silky strands to tumble all around her.

Her chest rose and fell faster and faster, her full breasts pushing against her white cotton shirt. Even her semi-uniform of the simple blouse and khakis she wore appeared elegant. She had a Scarlett Johansson–type lushness to her. No, his attraction to her hadn't dimmed one watt in the past year.

If anything, abstinence had made the gnawing hunger all the more fierce.

Desperate to regain his equilibrium, he searched for a subject that would put a damper on the chemistry crackling between them strong enough to start an in-flight accident. He raised his voice to be heard over her headphones. "How's your brother?"

Her violet-blue eyes snapped up from her book. She yanked out the ear buds. "I see you're as heartless as ever. My brother is still in the juvenile detention center where you put him."

Her brother had come to live with her when his parents had given up trying to control him. But the change of venue hadn't done a thing to alter the delinquent teen's attitude, and Timothy's behavior had begun to border on criminal. Finally, when Timothy had committed vandalism at a Medina resort where Javier oversaw security, there'd been no choice but for Javier to have him arrested.

He knew it had been the right decision, even if it had meant incurring Victoria's wrath. God, she was hot when she got mad.

"Your brother put himself in juvie by pretending to be a valet so he could take joyrides in high-priced cars, just to name one of his stunts that you dismiss as a 'prank.' I happen to call it criminal activity. Having people make excuses for him certainly doesn't help."

"Are you saying it's my fault he's in jail?" She slapped her book down. "I took that job in Boston to be closer to you and now I'm stuck there to be near my brother in jail. What do you think of that?"

"It does not matter what I think." He shrugged with a nonchalance he didn't feel. In fact, blood surged south as she leaned forward. "I am only here to do my job, as are you."

"My job?" She yanked her seat belt off and stood sharply, her signature temper sparking in her eyes. "Convenient that you're finally remembering that now. How about we stick to the professional and stop talking about my family?"

He nodded. Why had he provoked her with the reference to her brother? He wasn't sure. In fact, mentioning Timothy Palmer only made him angry about how much trouble the teen had caused his sister, the kind of danger he'd brought to Victoria's doorstep.

What Timothy had cost them all.

Victoria stood in the middle of the plane, glancing left and right as if searching for an escape hatch. Rather tough to find even on a luxury plane.

He gestured toward the back. "There's a bed if you wish to nap."

A bed? Not the smartest thing to mention with so much awareness searing the air.

Her eyes went wide with an answering arousal just as the plane bounced on a pocket of turbulence. He reached for her, but she jerked to the side, bracing a hand on the leather seat. The jet bucked again. Victoria's feet shot out from under her.

And she landed squarely in his lap.

Two

Her heart plunged to her stomach as the plane lurched and she landed in Javier's lap. She grabbed his shoulders before she toppled to the floor. The jet bounced along another pocket of turbulence, thrusting her against the solid wall of his muscular chest.

And the thick arousal straining against his pants.

Oh. My.

She searched his hot brown eyes and her skin tingled. The scent of him—bay rum and manly musk—triggered memories of the two of them tangled up naked together in bed. She knew well how much pleasure waited for her if she dared to ditch her panties, free his erection and straddle him here, now.

A year ago she would have done just that. After all, they were alone in the airplane cabin, the pilot ensconced behind the door. Javier had avowed he enjoyed her impetuous nature. She'd never told him how he drove her to cast aside sexual inhibitions in a way no other man had before.

Their affair had been filled with impulsive, uninhibited hookups. While making love, Javier shed his cool demeanor as quickly and fully as his clothes. The attraction between them had been combustible, distracting them from the differences they'd both tried so hard to ignore.

But those differences had eventually—inevitably—driven them apart, shattering her heart in the process. She reminded herself that nothing had changed.

She wriggled to slide free of the man, the temptation.

He clamped onto her hips, his jaw tight. "Victoria, for God's sake, hold still."

His ragged request turned her shaky knees even weaker. His mouth was a mere whisper away. So easily she could angle her lips against his and without question the flames would ignite.

Less than a half hour in his company and she was already prepared to repeat the same mistakes.

She sagged against his chest even as her mouth demanded, "Let me go."

"I'm trying." His fingers twitched against her hips. With restraint? Or frustrated desire? "Believe me, woman, I am trying."

The heat of his words flowed over her face, soaked into her soul, which had hungered for him so very desperately this past year. Why did he have to be here? Now? For the past year in Boston, she'd half feared, half hoped she would run into him on the street. He worked on Martha's Vineyard for his Medina cousin, but it wasn't that far away.

As the anniversary of their breakup approached, she'd known she had to do something to get him out of her heart once and for all. The temporary stint subbing for Enrique Medina's regular nurse had seemed like a sign, a chance to prove to herself that she could now walk in Javier Cortez's world unscathed.

But this plane ride had proven that she couldn't. Only, she couldn't afford to back out, not when she so desperately needed the money to pay her brother's lawyer for the appeal that could free him on his eighteenth birthday rather than his twenty-first.

She also couldn't afford to forget for a minute that Javier was the one who'd put her brother behind bars for what amounted to a series of teenage pranks.

Tears stung her eyes and before she could hide them, Javier knuckled one away with surprising tenderness. God, having his hands on her again was heaven and hell.

The sound system crackled a split second's warning before the pilot's voice filled the luxurious space. "The weather isn't cooperating with us today. We have storms ahead for most of our trip. Please return to your seats and fasten your seat belts."

Javier's hands slid enticingly down her arms before settling on her hips again as he lifted her. But he didn't let go. His steadying grip stayed on her waist.

She braced her palms against his chest, a hard wall as unyielding as the man. "Javier." Her voice was so shaky she cleared her throat and tried again. "When we arrive at the island, I think it best that we avoid each other."

"If you have no feelings for me, then seeing each

other isn't a problem." His fingers skimmed up her spine, drawing her closer.

"Of course I have feelings for you." She kept her hands on his chest, her arms maintaining at least a modicum of distance between them. She put ice into her words. "You infuriate me. It hurts my heart just to look at you. I hate the way my body seems to want you in spite of everything. But I am a nurse. I understand it's just biology."

"I would call it chemistry." His eyes smoldered.

"Chemistry notwithstanding, I don't want you in my life. So I would appreciate it if you would please keep your distance."

He stared into her eyes for so long she feared he would argue. Or maybe even kiss her, which would only prove just how quickly chemistry would trump her logic.

Finally his hands fell away and he let her go. "It's a large island. The king's mansion is huge. Staying apart shouldn't be any problem at all—although you're free to let me know if you change your mind."

As she made her way across the aisle, she watched him calmly pull a laptop from his briefcase as if she didn't even exist. How could he compartmentalize his emotions so easily?

Her legs folded under her and she dropped into her seat, her body still on fire from the feel of Javier's hands.

Javier went through the motions of working on his computer, but his real focus was the woman across the aisle from him. She'd given up trying to read and had fallen into a fitful sleep. Dark circles stained the delicate skin under her eyes, attesting to long-term strain. Most likely caused by that damn fool brother of hers. Javier had hoped putting the kid on the road to reform would ease the pressure on his sister. He'd tracked the boy's behavior since Timothy entered the juvenile detention center and the teen seemed to be keeping his nose clean.

Javier had kept track of Victoria, too, which made it all the more surprising to find her here today. He should have known, damn it.

Could the aging king—his uncle—have set him up? The ailing man was physically near death, but his mind was still sharp as ever.

If so, Javier didn't appreciate being manipulated. If he wanted Victoria in his life again, then he would take action.

A niggling voice in his head reminded him of all the times he'd covertly watched over her in the past months. He'd been living his life in limbo. Very atypical for him. But then, the way he felt around Victoria was far from "typical."

Without a doubt, he had unfinished business with this woman. And he had a weeklong window at his uncle's island to find closure....

Or find his way back into her bed.

Three

Victoria stared out the small round window as finally, finally the flight neared an end. Between the crummy weather and the looming presence of Javier across the aisle, her nerves were knotted tightly. At least she would have work to occupy her soon.

In the distance, an island rested in the middle of the murky ocean. The storm front gave the world a fuzzy haze that deepened as night began to fall. Palm trees spiked from the landscape, lushly thick and so very different from the leafless snowy winter that gripped Boston.

She'd been to the island before, but the magnitude of it still threatened to steal her breath anew. The Medina compound was a small city unto itself, a surprise splash of lights in a sea so vast, like a holiday design on the water left past the season.

As the plane powered through the bumpy airspace,

the island began to take shape. A dozen or so small outbuildings dotted a semicircle around a massive structure—the main house bathed in floodlights.

The white mansion faced the ocean in a U-shape, constructed around a large courtyard with a pool. She could distinguish few details in the encroaching dark, but she recalled from her earlier visit how highly protected the place was—a gilded cage for Enrique Medina's sons, to say the least. Even from a distance she couldn't miss the grand scale of the sprawling estate, the sort befitting royalty.

Yet the former ruler chose to cut himself off from the top-notch medical facilities his fortune could so easily buy. She would do her best for him, but his critical condition would be better monitored in a hospital, something she intended to remind him of as politely and firmly as possible. Often.

She was here for Enrique Medina, and any problems with the deposed king's nephew needed to be put on hold. Her hormones needed to be put on hold.

The intercom system crackled a second before the pilot announced, "Attention please. We're anticipating a rough landing. Weather only worsens the longer we're in the air, so we're going to put this thing down on the ground as soon as possible. Prepare yourselves for a rapid descent."

Her heart bolted up into her throat. Before she could stop herself, she reached for Javier's hand.

Javier's hand was numb from how hard Victoria had squeezed it during the entire hazardous landing. He'd kept his calm, even though his own gut had twisted at the thought of her in danger.

Now safely on the ground, he held the umbrella over her head as they raced through the sheeting rain toward the Porsche Cayenne four-wheel drive waiting for them. He needed to get her inside the car and safely to the mansion.

He nodded to the armed security guards and waved for the Porsche to be brought closer.

Lightning split the inky sky. Thunder clapped fast on its heels. Too fast for his peace of mind. He hooked an arm around Victoria's waist and pulled her to his side. His feet pounded faster on the paved lot alongside the airstrip, each step splashing in deeper puddles as the downpour increased.

He yanked open the passenger door and guided her inside before racing around the hood to settle behind the wheel and start the SUV. The finely tuned engine purred to life as guards loaded the luggage in back.

Seconds later Javier steered out of the parking area and onto the narrow two-lane road lined with palm trees.

Victoria plucked at her soaked khakis. "I feel awful dripping water all over such an incredible car."

He cranked up the heater. There was a nip in the air despite the subtropical climes, worsened by the damp of the rain. "No worries about the water. The car's just a thing."

"To you, maybe. To me, this sucker costs more than I make in a year."

"The seats will survive a little water." Although his sanity might not survive the sight of her soaked to the skin, her nipples pressing against her shirt. The white blouse had gone sheer when wet, giving him a too-clear view of her lace bra.

"Eyes on the road, please."

"Right." He looked away fast, mentally kicking himself for becoming distracted, especially in such crummy weather. The Porsche's top-of-the-line shocks worked double-time to absorb the bumps of rolling over downed branches littering the road.

But his mind kept returning to what Victoria had said about the Porsche. He'd never considered that his family's money might make her uncomfortable. His portion of the royal cache was in the millions, but he'd chosen to earn his way in the world, to have a profession. He'd assumed he and Victoria had that work ethic in common, and now he realized she'd never thought anything of the sort.

Lightning ripped the sky in half just as a realization thundered through his brain. What else had he missed about Victoria while he was too caught up in the incredible sex to look deeper?

The sky lit up again. A crack sounded, differently this time.

"Damn!" He jerked the SUV left. Hard. Right when a towering tree split in half.

The Porsche skidded sideways to a stop just shy of the tree as it crashed across the road in front of them. Rain hammered the rooftop, the only sound in the aftermath.

He turned fast. "Victoria?"

"I'm okay," she said.

Her face was pale, but otherwise she seemed unharmed.

"Thank heavens you reacted so quickly, Javier. Now we can just take an alternative route."

Alternative route? If only it could be that simple. He

knew this island like the back of his hand. He had to in order to keep the Medina family safe.

"There is no other road to the house from here. We're going to have to turn back."

Her eyes went wide with dawning shock. "But the king? He's waiting for me."

"He will have to make do with a mansion full of staff and an entire clinic at his disposal. And his other nurse won't leave until you arrive." His mind churned with options…and enticing possibilities. Hadn't he wanted to find closure with her? Maybe he just needed to get her out of his system. "We should get somewhere safe and dry soon."

Somewhere alone.

She eyed him suspiciously. "Where?"

"No worries. I know every inch of this island."

Because he'd just decided on the perfect place to take Victoria to have her all to himself.

Four

Victoria shivered inside her wet clothes even with the SUV's heater blasting. Her skin still tingled from the way Javier had devoured her with his eyes. And now they would be spending the night together, whether she liked it or not.

He was on his cell phone informing the main house of their status so the king wouldn't worry.

"Right," Javier answered the person on the other end of the line, his Bluetooth headset glowing in his ear. "Since the road is blocked, we're going to hole up at the greenhouse for the night. No need to risk sending anybody after us now that you've hunkered down for the storm.... Of course...I'm sure.... I'll check in first thing tomorrow."

And that fast, he ended the call as if it was nothing more than a business dealing—rather than sealing their fate. Sealing them together, alone, for the next twelve hours. How would she resist him? Suddenly the air felt altogether too hot. Her body flushed with desire.

Decelerating, Javier rounded a corner, leaving behind the road and lines of towering palms and entering a clearing. Headlamps striped over the glass structure of the greenhouse. Only a small gazebo and a sprawling oak stood between them and the conservatory.

He pulled up beside the front door, turned off the engine and twisted toward her. "This is the greenhouse I told you about. It also has a café area, so we should be able to find something to eat. There's even a sofa and shower in the back office."

She drew in a deep, bracing breath and reached for the door handle. "Then I guess we should head inside." Racing out before he could come around with the umbrella, she sprinted toward the front entrance. Rain pelted her skin. Javier charged alongside her up the stone steps that led inside. He threw open the double doors, startling a sparrow into flight in the otherwise deserted building.

As he closed the door, a cloak of darkness and heavily perfumed air enveloped her.

Slowly her eyes adapted until shadowy images took shape. In contrast to the crowded nurseries she'd visited in the past, this space sprawled like an indoor floral park, and included gathering areas and benches for reading or meditation. Lush ferns dangled overhead. Tiered racks of florist's buckets with cut flowers stretched along a far wall. Potted palms and cacti added height to the interior landscape. An Italian marble fountain trickled below a darkened skylight.

Water spilled softly from a carved snake's mouth as it curled around some reclining Roman god.

She spun slowly in the cavernous room, immersing herself in the thickly intoxicating scents. Vines grew tangled and dense over the windows. Moonlight filtered through the glass roof, muted by rivulets of rain. "This island has everything."

She shouldn't have been surprised—the island had not only medical and dental clinics, but a chapel, guesthouses and stables.

And a very sexy man who was all hers for the night. Amber moonbeams streaked over his broad shoulders. His jet-black hair glinted with raindrops, calling to her fingers to skim over his head with the familiarity they'd once shared.

"Everything? Very close. My uncle did his damnedest to give his three sons a 'normal' childhood after they left San Rinaldo, as much as he could, short of letting them off the island. The king wanted to make sure his family had everything so they wouldn't want to leave."

She slowed in front of him, feeling the weight of Javier's gaze as he stopped beside wrought-iron screens twined with hydrangeas and morning glories.

"What about you?" she asked.

"I grew up in Argentina," he answered, his handsome face impassive. "We were the decoy family. We may be cousins, but we looked enough like the Medinas for the king's purposes."

She gasped in horror. "How awful."

"My family was only alive because he financed our escape." He stroked a hydrangea bloom nonchalantly.

"The danger we faced in Argentina was less than anything here."

Victoria approached him warily. How had she not learned this about him? She should have pressed him about his background once they grew serious, but there was so much secrecy around his family and he'd insisted she was safer not knowing.

Now that the Medina secret had been revealed to the world by Javier's cousin Alys, however, there were fewer restraints. Maybe now she could understand him better, find a way to make peace with their heartbreaking relationship.

Thinking of Alys, she said, "After being forced into seclusion, used to divert danger, it's easy to see how your cousin might resent the Medinas."

"Don't try to justify what Alys did." The vine snapped between his fingers abruptly, his fist crushing the bloom. "She betrayed the Medinas by leaking their secret to the press. Alys is not as closely related to the king and his sons as I am. She hoped to marry a prince and gain all the perks and the fame that came with it. Only the worst kind of person betrays family for money."

"Just like my brother?" She took a step toward him, anger sparking. "Is that what you're trying to say?"

His chin tipped—stubborn, uncompromising. "Read into my words what you will."

"I really hate it when you do that." She plucked at her clammy clothes, her skin hot and too tight for her body. Damn him for the way he unsettled her.

"Do what?" He towered over her.

"Never answer my questions." She stood her ground. She knew he'd never harm her the way he'd crushed that fragile bloom in his fist. "Why can't you ditch the whole regal air and simply give me a straight answer?"

He studied her for so long she wondered if he might just walk away, ignore her altogether. Then something shifted in his expression, his brown eyes turning smoky.

"Because—" he slid his hand up to cup her cheek, the hydrangea petals soft and fragrant between his palm and her face "—when you stand so close to me, I can only think of kissing you."

Five

Javier had known he had to kiss Victoria from the second he saw her spinning under the skylight, muted moonbeams washing over her. The way she embraced life had drawn him to her from the start.

Now she stood only a breath away. Her tongue peeking out and touching her top lip was all the encouragement he needed to follow through. He slid a knuckle under her chin and tipped her face to his. After a year apart, a year of aching to have her, she was in his arms again.

Pulling her to him, he sealed his mouth to hers as she opened for him with a sigh that tasted of pure Victoria. Raw desire seared through his veins, firing hard and low.

She looped her arms around his neck and arched against him. Her damp clothes clung to his, fabric warmed from her body. From their passion.

He delved deeper into her mouth, relearning the feel of her, the texture, what made her respond and wriggle closer. Her breasts pressed against his chest, stirring memories of his hands curved around their creamy softness. The pounding storm overhead echoed the drumming of his pulse in his ears.

His hands stroked down her back, then lower until he cupped her bottom to bring her more fully against the length of him. "God, Victoria, I want you so damn much it hurts."

"I know," she whispered against his mouth. "I feel the same way. It's been too long. A whole year without you, without this..."

Her hand slipped between them and over his arousal. His head fell back, his eyes sliding closed. He ground his teeth in restraint until he feared he'd crack a crown. He drew in a bracing breath. The scent of her fabric softener released by the rain mingled with the heavy floral scent of the conservatory, drugging him.

He'd chosen the greenhouse deliberately. It was the most private and romantic locale he could think of at a moment's notice. He could have pushed for the local head of security to send someone to retrieve them. But he couldn't give up the opportunity to be alone with Victoria.

Suddenly a horrible thought occurred to him.... He'd manipulated her, brought her here without explaining there were alternatives, without giving her a choice. He hadn't been fair. He might be autocratic, but he prided himself on his integrity. Even when it had cost him her love last year. Even if it cost him this second chance.

Gripping her shoulders, he eased away with more

than a little regret. She swayed under his hands, her eyes fluttering open to reveal dazed desire and a hint of confusion.

"Javier?" She fisted her fingers in the lapels of his damp suit coat.

He skimmed a strand of her blond hair from her face. "There's never been any question how much we want each other. But we need to be honest."

"You want to talk? Now?" Her voice rose with incredulity.

His libido echoed her objection. But if they were going to take this further, he had to be up front with her. "We don't have to stay here tonight. I can make a call and have someone take us to the mansion."

"But the storm? I thought the roads were blocked?"

"The main roads are out, yes. But there are some four-wheel-drive options. The weather makes things difficult, but not impossible."

Realization slid over her face, her eyes going wide. "You're saying you brought me here on purpose?"

Was she angry? He couldn't tell. At least she hadn't pulled away, so he pressed on.

"Yes, I chose this place so that we would be alone together. I planned to romance you with flowers." He plucked a hydrangea petal from her hair. "All the same, that kiss caught me by surprise…."

"Me, too," she admitted wryly.

"I also didn't expect how fast things would spiral out of control between us. Though I should have anticipated it, given our past." He cupped her face and held her gaze with his. "If we go beyond one kiss, if we stay here for the night, I need you to be one hundred percent certain it's what you want."

She stared at him for so long he prepared himself for the increasing possibility that she would turn him away. And this time it would be for good. There would be no more chances with her. This woman, her beautiful blue eyes, her scent, her touch, would haunt him for the rest of his life.

She unfurled her fingers from his suit coat, and regret slammed through him so damn hard he almost rocked back on his soaked heels. Could he really let her go again?

She dusted her hands along his jacket, brushing off more hydrangea petals that clung to the fabric. And he realized she wasn't pushing him away at all. In fact, her hips were nestling closer in a perfect fit against him.

"Javier—" she stroked her finger along his neck to his jaw "—no one should drive in this weather when we have a safe place to stay. I am exactly where I want to be."

Relief flooded him, more than he expected. He knew there were still more things they should discuss, more issues to be aired and resolved....

Like the full extent of the role he'd played in her brother's incarceration.

She sketched her fingertips along his lips. "Let's stop talking and make the most of this night together. We'll deal with the rest tomorrow when the storm clears."

He couldn't miss the surety in her voice. And while he questioned the wisdom of letting sex distract them as it had so often in the past, he couldn't resist this opportunity to be with her.

Extending his hand, Javier stepped back toward

the office, which he happened to know conveniently housed a shower. "I think it's time we got out of these wet clothes."

Six

Victoria fit her hand in Javier's, committing to the moment. She pushed aside thoughts of the times she'd harbored dreams of committing her life and heart to him, as well.

Tonight they would make love again. She hadn't forgiven him for what he'd done to her brother, but she couldn't deny herself this chance to be with Javier, to ease the ache that had been building for an entire year.

She needed to have one last time with him. Although there weren't a lot of flat surfaces here to choose from. "Where are we going?"

Leaves brushed her legs as she walked past a climbing vine.

He smiled, his dark eyes lit with promise. "The office has a full bathroom. I have fond memories of how we used to shower together."

"This place has a tub?" Her thumb grazed the inside

of his wrist along his strong, steady pulse as she envisioned floating rose petals.

"Gardening can be messy business." He backed her around a potting station with terra-cotta urns in a neat line, bags of soil stacked under the table.

"Makes sense, I guess. And wonderfully smart of you to think of that."

He reached beyond her to open the office door. "If I was as smart as you give me credit for, I would have thought of this long ago."

"Shhhh..." She pressed a finger to his mouth. "No more talking."

She replaced her finger with her lips, and thank heaven he took the hint. His hands returned to her body, making fast work of the buttons down her blouse. And she had no intention of lagging behind. She skimmed off his jacket, her hands remembering how best to undress him, until their clothes left a trail into the bathroom.

Skin to skin, she fitted herself more fully against his body, sighing with a deep satisfaction from just the feel of him. With another sigh she let her head loll back, and she looked around them....

Wow...this wasn't just some tiny powder room.

Her eyes took in the tan travertine tiles, the thick towels and, most important, the spacious spa shower with an assortment of floral soaps stacked on shelves built into the wall.

Her visions of floating roses shifted to fantasies of lathering each other with soap flecked with lilac, gardenia, jasmine or honeysuckle. "I just wouldn't have expected anything so luxurious in a greenhouse."

"My uncle does not scrimp." He reached past her to turn on the water.

She trailed her fingers down Javier's bare chest, reveling in the flex of muscles under her touch. "No complaints here. One last question..." Her stomach twisted in apprehension. "Do you have birth control? We didn't exactly plan for this."

"I have it taken care of," he vowed. "I would never leave you unprotected. The bathroom on the corporate jet is fully stocked, and when we were on the plane I took what we might need." He bent to snag his pants from the floor and dipped a hand into his pocket. "I didn't want to be caught unprepared."

"Thank goodness." She stood in the open shower, one hand braced on the wall. "How many did you bring?"

He devoured her with his eyes as he backed her inside and placed the stack of packets in the soap dish. "Ambitious plenty."

Warm pellets of water sluiced over her naked body, but his bold confidence seduced her even more. "For once, I like your arrogance."

Their bodies melded under the heated spray, which was pooling around their feet. She kissed, nipped and sipped along his neck, along his shoulders. His hands were all over her, so perfectly stroking her breasts in just the right places she realized he hadn't forgotten a second of their time together, either.

Then he soaped up a lather between his palms, the scent of lilac clinging to the steam so potently she was sure that fresh flowers were pressed into the bars. And then he drove all thought away as his fingers slicked between her legs.

She rediscovered his body as fully as he explored hers until she thought she would shatter, right there, right then in his arms. “I need you inside me. No more waiting.”

His low growl of approval rumbled against her chest. She barely registered how quickly he sheathed himself, and in an instant he had her against the tiled wall. Cupping her behind the knees, he lifted her, hooking her legs around his waist until he was perfectly positioned to…thrust.

She hugged him closer, dug her heels tighter into his flanks as he moved and she met him. They synced, reclaiming their rhythm as the past twelve months evaporated with the steam. As if all those nights she'd lain alone in her bed hungry for him hadn't happened. As if she hadn't dreamed of having him just this way.

Except with those dreams, she never finished. She woke unfulfilled, aching and lonely for him. There had been so many good times before the end….

She pushed away thoughts of her brother, of her horrible last argument with Javier, and focused on the feel of him within her, his arms and impassioned words all around her. His hard, muscled chest brushed against her breasts, the light rasp of hair teasing her to pebbly tight peaks.

The gathering need tingled inside her, prickling along her skin, hotter than the water vaporizing around them until… Her release rocked through her, showered through her, pulsing again and again just as he did.

His hoarse shout of completion twined with hers and she could have sworn the ground vibrated around them. Maybe it was more thunder, but regardless, she'd been rocked by the force of their coming together.

Her legs slowly slid down to the tile floor again, but she doubted she could have stood on her own. She held on, her face buried in his neck as he gathered her closer.

She couldn't hide from the truth any longer. Being with Javier was different, special. She would always want him, the man who had demanded she do the one thing she never could.

Turn her back on her brother.

Seven

Inhaling the scent of flowers, Victoria and their love-making, Javier pulled her closer to his side on the makeshift bed on the floor under the skylight. After their shower, he'd found some blankets and pulled pillows from the sofa. They'd made love throughout the night, catnapping in between.

Well, she napped. He watched her sleep, a pleasure he'd missed over the past year.

And now their night was coming to an end and he had to act decisively to make her his, because he couldn't walk away from her again. He nuzzled the top of her head, savoring the silky texture of her hair splashed across his chest.

The rain had stopped; the sun was just beginning to pinken the horizon.

Victoria stirred against him and sighed. "We should get dressed soon."

"We should. And we will." Sometime before dawn he'd put on his trousers and run out to retrieve their suitcases from the Porsche. Then he'd quickly gotten naked with her again. He trailed his fingers along her silky arm. "But just because we're leaving this place, you have to know I won't let you go as easily this time."

Avoiding his eyes, she slid her leg over his intimately. "Let's talk about something else. Let's do something else."

He clamped a hand on her thigh, forcing down his body's instinctive reaction to her nearness. "Why are you really on the island? You had to realize I would hear you'd returned, even if we didn't run into each other."

She pulled away. "Are you accusing me of setting this up?"

"No need to get bristly." He grazed his hand up to her waist. "I'm glad we had this night together."

She tugged the silky afghan around her and walked to the edge of the fountain, where he'd placed their suitcases. "I'm here because I didn't have any other way of making enough money to pay my brother's lawyer."

"You're here for your brother?" His body chilled. He sat up, following her with his eyes.

"Your uncle offered me a temporary fill-in job." She opened her paisley bag and tugged out a stack of clothing, her movements fast and jerky. "He said there aren't many nurses he trusts, especially since the Medina secret was splashed all over the papers."

"Your parents should be taking care of your brother's expenses." And if they hadn't given up and dumped their son in her lap, life would have been so different for all of them. "I'm only trying to protect you."

"He's my brother." She yanked on pink panties and a bra with quick, angry hands. "Family means something to me."

"Are you making a dig at my cousin?" He would have stood and walked over to her, but he was still too damned turned on by her. "I can't trust her, and I refuse to justify that to you."

She pulled on a fresh pair of khakis and a white button-up before sagging to sit on the bench around the fountain. Sighing, she put her face in her hands. "Would you please put some clothes on? My brain short-circuits when you're naked."

Now, that was a victory at least. He silently shoved himself to his feet and tugged on slacks and a shirt. "You can open your eyes."

She peered between her fingers with a begrudging smile. "Okay, I'll acknowledge your point. Your cousin is a security risk to the rest of your family, but she's also an adult. Timothy is a teenager." Standing, she faced him, ready to go toe-to-toe. "If his whole family walks away, who will he turn to?"

He gripped her arms. "That's my whole point, damn it!"

"What do you mean?"

He pivoted away sharply, stunned at how she'd knocked him off his game so easily. "Forget I said anything."

"I can't do that." She stepped around in front of him, her hands on her hips. Her jaw jutted stubbornly. "I will not abandon him, no matter what he does."

He could see she wasn't going to back down, even if she followed her brother right into harm's way.

And for the first time, he considered that he might have played a role in that by not telling her everything that had happened around her brother's arrest. He'd been trying to protect her.… And he'd royally screwed up.

He had to fix that, starting now. "Your brother wasn't guilty of just simple vandalism." He pushed out the truth he knew would crush her, but it would also keep her safe. "Victoria, he was part of a street gang."

"A gang?" She gasped in horror, in shock. She held up a hand of denial and backed away. "That's not true."

"Yes, it is." He started to reach for her, to comfort her, but her eyes stopped him short. He stuffed his hands into his pockets. "His lawyer knew it, because I gave him the proof. Surveillance cameras picked it up. He was being pressured to commit those acts—stealing cars, lifting jewelry—as initiation."

"Why wasn't I told any of this?" Anger snapped in her eyes.

Clearly any answer he gave to that was only going to make her angrier, so he deflected with "Why do you think his lawyer and I cut a deal? I wanted your brother safely tucked away. Your parents couldn't handle him, and you have to face that you couldn't, either. He was out of control. Juvenile detention wasn't just the place he deserved to be, it was the safest place for him to be."

Her lips pursed tight, her body rigid. "What gave you the right to decide all of that without consulting me? Obviously you didn't trust me.…" She held up her hand. "Never mind. Let's put this conversation on hold. This is all too much, too fast, and I'm too…mad and confused to even speak to you. The rain has stopped. We should leave."

He saw the determination in her eyes and couldn't help but admire how hard she fought for Timothy, how she put herself on the line for people she cared about. She was fiery and fearless, impetuous and idealistic in a way that touched him, no matter how much those qualities could stir trouble for her. And for him, too.

Yes, he could read her eyes well. While she was willing to forgive her brother anything, she wasn't so willing to extend that forgiveness to him.

What a damned inconvenient time to realize just how much he loved her.

Eight

Victoria held back her tears all the way to the Medina compound. Hurt, anger and betrayal warred inside her as she stood in front of the massive front doors. How could Javier have kept something so important from her?

And how could her brother have gotten himself tangled up with such a dangerous group without her having a clue?

Her head was spinning so fast she barely registered the lush landscape, the towering Spanish-style mansion she'd first seen over a year ago. She could think only of the man standing stonily beside her. How could she even consider renewing their relationship when he was every bit as intractable as ever?

And yet realizing how much harder it would be to walk away from him a second time made the tears burn even hotter behind her eyelids.

Before she could blink her vision clear again, the butler directed them to go around back where the king waited on the veranda. She walked alongside Javier on the landscaped path, past the pool in the courtyard. The citrus scent of orange trees heavy with fruit hung in the air. She rounded a corner, passing armed guards just before she spotted Enrique Medina.

Confined to a wheelchair, he was thin, gray and weary. Still, no matter the sallow pallor and thinner frame, Enrique's face was that of royalty. His aristocratic nose and chiseled jaw spoke of his ages-old warrior heritage. And while his heavy blue robe with emerald-green silk lapels was not the garb of a king in his prime, the rich fabrics and sleek leather slippers reflected his wealth.

Enrique greeted them both with a regal nod, then turned to his nephew. "Javier, could you walk down to the beach for a moment?" It was more of a demand than a request, his Spanish accent as thick as she remembered. "I wish to speak privately with Victoria. You and I can talk later."

Javier raised an eyebrow before pivoting away toward the beach—leaving her alone with the deposed king. Victoria couldn't help but notice how Javier purposefully retreated now after her demand that they not discuss her brother. She needed time, and from the way he'd accepted the old king's dictate without comment, she sensed Javier was giving her that space.

Sea breeze wrapping around her, she stepped forward, already assessing Enrique's health from a professional perspective. She hadn't received an update from the previous nurse yet, but the patchwork of veins prominent on the backs of his hands told her he'd been receiving IV medications often. "How are you feeling, sir?"

"Still stubborn about calling me Enrique, I see." His body might be weak, but his voice still commanded attention—it was as firm and constant as the roar of the waves crashing against the shore. "Thank you for agreeing to come."

She forced her focus to stay on him rather than on the man striding along the shore. "I am so very sorry you still require nursing care."

He waved aside her words of sympathy. "Have you and Javier made up?"

Her gaze snapped firmly to Enrique. "Pardon?"

"You spent the whole flight and last night together. I would hope the two of you have stopped being fools and repaired your relationship."

A suspicion flickered in her brain. With her nerves so raw, she blurted, "Did you send for me just so I would be with Javier?"

He lifted a gray eyebrow. "Even I cannot command the weather. But yes, I arranged things so you were on the same flight. I am running out of time to see my nephew settled. Something needed to be done."

Indignation starched her spine. She'd had her fill of this royal family maneuvering her life without consulting her. "What made you assume it was your place to do that, sir?"

Gripping the arms of his wheelchair, he sat up straighter. "Because I was once young and foolish. I thought I had forever to be with the woman I loved." He studied her with piercing brown eyes that reminded her of his nephew. "Sit down and stop looking at me as if I am the enemy."

His autocratic tone took as much getting used to now as it had last year, but she read the genuine caring in his eyes. The older man was dying and wanted to ensure that the people he loved were happy.

Slowly she took the seat across from him. "I'm listening."

"Good." He nodded regally. "If you and Javier don't have feelings for each other, then I have done nothing more than give you the chance to reflect on a past romance."

Her eyes trekked to Javier standing on the shore with his hands in his pockets, tall and handsome against the sunrise.

"Yes, I have…feelings for him…." She loved him. God, how she loved him, so deeply it had haunted her for the past year.

"He fears for your safety, you know, and with cause."

"My brother—"

"No… Javier is overprotective because of the way he was forced to grow up, always watching over our shoulder. Our family has been on the run, living in seclusion under assumed names for so long. It is difficult to throw aside those fears just because the world now has learned our secret."

Unbidden, images of Javier living as part of a decoy family for the Medinas came to mind. He had put himself in harm's way for the sake of family. Hardly the kind of man she could accuse of not caring about his relations. Regret for that comment she'd snapped at him niggled along her conscience.

Her heart ached for the young boy Javier had been, for the way it had marked the man he was today. "How do I get through those walls he has built around himself?"

He patted her arm. "My dear, be tenacious with him, just as you are tenacious when it comes to your brother."

His words sank in, bringing so much of her relationship with Javier into focus. She'd fought for her brother, was willing to forgive him even his criminal behavior. Yet she hadn't fought for her relationship with Javier, a man who'd gone to the mat for her family. For so long she'd been able to depend only on herself, her parents letting her down—letting her brother down—again and again. Somewhere along the line she'd forgotten how to trust, and how to work as a team.

Her eyes sought Javier, the man who'd offered her everything. The time had come for her to be brave enough, bold enough to fight for him.

Javier watched Victoria stride down the beach toward him, her shoes in her hand, the wind streaking her long blond hair behind her. God, he wanted her with him, always. He would never give up trying to persuade her, but he understood that ultimately the decision had to be hers. He'd powered his way through life up until now, but steamrolling this woman wasn't fair—and it wouldn't work.

She stopped alongside him, staring out over the ocean.

He studied her for some sign of what scrolled through her mind. "What did my uncle have to say?"

A smile tugged her full lips. "That he brought us both here to work out our problems."

Not surprising. The king structured his world obsessively as if he could protect them all still. Javier had always admired his uncle's wisdom, the caution he exercised to protect his family. "I suspected as much. Sorry about the whole royal take-charge thing. It's in our blood."

She laughed softly. "Only you would apologize for being related to a king."

"Only you wouldn't give a damn that my family is royal and obscenely wealthy." He had never once needed to wonder if she cared about him because of his family tree.

"Actually," she said, "I'm glad your uncle did it."

Now, that did surprise him. "Even though I'm still the same jerk I was a year ago?"

She turned to face him, scraping back the windswept hair that streamed over her cheeks. "You're not a jerk. Assertive sometimes, but I'm beginning to understand that everything you do is for others."

While he didn't totally buy into her altruistic picture of him, he sure as hell wasn't going to argue. "Victoria—" His voice sounded ragged even to his own ears. "I need you in my life."

"Damn straight you do." She slid her hand into his and squeezed. "I think the separation was as tough on you as it was on me. Last year you wouldn't have admitted to taking me to the greenhouse on purpose. You gave me an out if I wanted it."

"It wasn't easy." An understatement, to say the least. He gathered her against his chest and inhaled the scent of her shampoo, the scent of her. "More than anything I want us to be together, not living even a couple of hours apart. I like my job in Martha's Vineyard, but

I have the financial security to go elsewhere if you're intent on staying in Boston—"

She placed her fingers over his lips. "I don't want us to spend even one more day apart. I'm a nurse. I can work anywhere you are, and Martha's Vineyard is still close enough for me to help my brother get his act together."

Her brother. Her family. His family now, too, through Victoria.

He looked back up at the mansion, the U-shape layout wrapping around them, a protective cocoon of family present to help them resolve their differences and find the happiness they'd struggled to capture on their own. Being a Medina might have come with strings attached, but they were also the kind of ties that tethered him. Grounded him.

She curled her arms around his waist and pressed her cheek against his chest. "What are we going to do about my brother?"

"We?" He tipped her face up. "That's the first time you've asked for my help, you know."

"I can't give up on my brother, but I admit, my old way of dealing with his problems wasn't effective." She looped her arms around his neck. "Perhaps we could talk through some tough-love alternatives for him. We could work together. You don't have to carry the worries of the whole world all by yourself. And neither do I anymore, thanks to you."

He smiled. "I can definitely live with that. On one condition..."

"And that would be?"

Looking into her beautiful blue eyes, Javier said the words he'd been waiting to share since the day he'd met her. “Marry me. Be my wife, my lover, the mother of my children. Share your life with me so I can show you every single day just how very much I love you.”

Her smile shone brighter than the sun rising over the ocean. “Yes, yes, yes and a million times yes to everything. I love you and will marry you, and I look forward to waking up with you every morning for the rest of my life.”

He sealed his mouth to Victoria’s as firmly as he sealed his promise of forever loving her.

* * * * *

PASSION

Desire

COMING NEXT MONTH

AVAILABLE APRIL 10, 2012

#2149 FEELING THE HEAT

The Westmorelands

Brenda Jackson

Dr. Micah Westmoreland knows Kalina Daniels hasn't forgiven him. But he can't ignore the heat that still burns between them....

#2150 ON THE VERGE OF I DO

Dynasties: The Kincaids

Heidi Betts

#2151 HONORABLE INTENTIONS

Billionaires and Babies

Catherine Mann

#2152 WHAT LIES BENEATH

Andrea Laurence

#2153 UNFINISHED BUSINESS

Cat Schield

#2154 A BREATHLESS BRIDE

The Pearl House

Fiona Brand

Taft Bowman knew he'd ruined any chance he'd had for happiness with Laura Pendleton when he drove her away years ago...and into the arms of another man, thousands of miles away. Now she was back, a widow with two small children...and despite himself, he was starting to believe in second chances.

A younger woman stood there, and from this distance he had only a strange impression, as though she was somehow standing on an island of calm amid the chaos of the scene, the flashing lights of the emergency vehicles, shouts between his crew members, the excited buzz of the crowd.

And then the woman turned and he just about tripped over a snaking fire hose somebody shouldn't have left there.

Laura.

He froze, and for the first time in fifteen years as a firefighter, he forgot about the incident, his mission, just what the hell he was doing here.

Laura.

Ten years. He hadn't seen her in all that time, since the week before their wedding when she had given him back his ring and left town. Not just town. She had left the whole damn country, as if she couldn't run far enough to get away from him.

Some part of him desperately wanted to think he had made some kind of mistake. It couldn't be her. That was just some other slender woman with a long sweep of honey-blond hair and big, blue, unforgettable eyes. But no. It was definitely Laura. Sweet and lovely.

Not his.

He was going to have to go over there and talk to her. He didn't want to. He wanted to stand there and pretend he hadn't seen her. But he was the fire chief. He couldn't hide out just because he had a painful history with the daughter of the property owner.

Sometimes he hated his job.

Will Taft and Laura be able to make the years recede…or is the gulf between them too broad to ever cross?

Find out in
A COLD CREEK REUNION
Available April 2012 from Harlequin® Special Edition® wherever books are sold.

HSEEXP0412